THE ST
TURNE

Any standoff could not prove favorable to SLAM, and Slater ordered an immediate fighting pullout.

"Let's do it now!" he yelled, and pointed toward the main refinery building. "Use satchel charges."

While Hawke and Bishop covered him, Slater set the charges for a twenty-second delay and hurled two of the musette bags filled with high explosives into the refinery building.

Flashes of white light strobed through the town square as the charges went off with a deafening bang. Blast overpressure sent tongues of fire licking out over the scorched-black masonry as pulses of energy thundered in the night. To a distance of thirty meters out from the epicenter of the blast, the earth trembled from the effects of the detonations.

But within seconds the booming of the charges had faded and another sound picked up the beat of destruction as the cadence of 7.62 mm small-arms fire filled the air.

DAN MATTHEWS

SLAM

Shadow
Warriors

A GOLD EAGLE BOOK FROM
W⚫RLDWIDE ®

TORONTO • NEW YORK • LONDON
AMSTERDAM • PARIS • SYDNEY • HAMBURG
STOCKHOLM • ATHENS • TOKYO • MILAN
MADRID • WARSAW • BUDAPEST • AUCKLAND

First edition December 1993.

ISBN 0-373-63409-9

Special thanks and acknowledgment to
David Alexander for his contribution to this work.

SHADOW WARRIORS

Shadow Warriors

PROLOGUE

Lines in the Sand

PROLOGUE

The bedouin scanned the horizon with eyes as alert as the desert falcon's. Though the mullahs in Tehran had decreed the activity he was engaged in to be a crime punishable by death, the bedouin was not concerned.

He was a Baluchi, a member of a fierce and ancient tribal people whose territory straddled Iran, Pakistan and Afghanistan, and a Sunni Muslim, as well.

He owed no allegiance to the Shiite clerics who ruled Iran and he went about his task with the blessing of his people, for whom the trafficking in heroin had long been a source of sustenance.

Such had been the way of the tribes who inhabited the region known as the Golden Crescent for centuries, and such would it continue despite the shifts in power politics that had brought sweeping changes to the Middle East.

The bedouin saw the three double flashes that came from headlights across the border, inside Afghanistan. He used a flashlight to signal back in kind.

Soon the Range Rover convoy came trundling along the dusty road that led down from the mountainous lands to the east.

Inside were hard-eyed men dressed in the garb of the Afghan *mujahedeen* and porting the Kalashnikov Avtomats prized by the Afghan guerrillas as symbols of manhood to complement the curved *jambiya* daggers they wore sheathed at their belts.

The guerrilla band with which they were affiliated was based near the Helmand River. On the flats straddling the river's fertile banks, opium-producing poppies were grown in abundance by the rebel forces who waged fierce jihad against the government in Kabul.

The revenue gained from traffic in the poppy and in the opium base produced from it went to purchase much-needed armament the rebels needed to continue their fight, for after the Soviet pullout their American patrons stopped supplying sophisticated arms and logistical support.

The bedouin waited patiently until the convoy had stopped. He dismounted his camel and strode to meet the guerrilla chieftain who walked toward him. They came close together and threw their arms around one another in the manner of Arabs.

"God is great," they intoned by way of the traditional salutation. Then they separated to consummate the business that had brought them to this desolate spot.

ELSEWHERE IN IRAN, another man received visitors at a villa on the heights overlooking the city of Tehran. The villa had belonged to members of the shah's royal family before the Iranian leader had been ousted by Shiite militants in 1979, ending the rule of the Pahlavis forever.

The newcomers stationed their bodyguards outside. Eyes behind mirrored sunglasses watched the meeting site perimeter carefully.

"The great leader of the revolution sends his heartfelt greetings," the host informed his guests. "He wishes me to advise you that I enjoy his full and complete support in this matter. Now come into my living chamber. We will talk there."

The guests were received by liveried servants. These were native Thais who didn't speak a word of Farsi or Arabic, and were specially imported to perform menial tasks throughout the Middle East. They worked long hours without complaint.

"They do not understand. Converse freely," the master of the house said in Arabic, a language that all his guests understood. His speech was tinged by a Spanish accent that betrayed his national origins.

The first speaker was a relative of Iranian President Hashemi Rafsanjani. He had been sent as the president's representative.

"Please communicate to the great leader that the Islamic Republic of Iran thanks him for the arrangements. We believe, furthermore, that our meeting heralds a new era of cooperation against our mutual enemies."

"It will be made known," the house owner stated.

All parties were aware that the man they referred to was the Libyan dictator Colonel Moammar Khaddaffi. Their host had resided in Libya for more than a decade, after sojourning in Syria, Russia, Czechoslovakia, East Germany and several other countries.

After the Berlin Wall came down, documents found in the headquarters of the former East German state security service, or Stasi, showed a record of his activities during the late eighties.

Copies of these documents had come into the possession of various spy networks including the Israeli Mossad. If he were to lose the protection he now enjoyed from his powerful patrons, the host knew the Mossad would kill him for the atrocities he had committed long ago with the Palestinian Black September Organization.

"As you know, the gulf war has forever changed the power relationships in the region," the relative of Rafsanjani said. "No longer can we play the Soviets against the Americans. Nor can we trust any other power in the region. We must be solely responsible for our own destiny. The new geopolitical reality demands this."

"I understand," replied the host, sipping strong coffee through a sugar cube as was the custom of the region. He knew all of this, but to say so outright would be to risk offending the president's representative. In the typical Middle Eastern fashion, his guests would come around to the point sooner or later.

"We have considered your proposal because we are in dire need of certain technological infrastructure in the field of nuclear energy," the second Iranian representative went on. The speaker was Nazir Fadlallah, Intelligence minister and head of the feared Iranian Intelligence service, Sawama. "These resources will be expensive," Fadlallah said.

"I understand fully," the host concurred, calling for more strong black coffee. "There will be no difficulties with the funds. Furthermore, they will be completely untraceable. You are not dealing with the boyish but treacherous American lieutenant colonel now, nor with his legion of fools. You are dealing with a professional and a man of honor."

"But do you really believe you can deliver as promised?" asked a fleshy-faced man in a dark business suit who was Baghdad's representative and a cousin of Saddam Hussein. "We had believed the old Istanbul-Marseilles heroin pipeline shut down long ago."

"And so, my friend, do Western law-enforcement personnel," replied their host with a grin. "But the original infrastructure remains in place. While the Americans turn their attention to the Cali Cartel and the Shan United Army, we can proceed without obstruction."

"But surely the channels—"

"—are still intact," the host cut in with a dismissive wave of his hand, anticipating the rest of the question. "Permit me to elaborate. The original Istanbul-Marseilles drug trafficking corridor—known popularly as the French Connection—was established after World War II. Its origins, indeed, have interesting parallels in contemporary events.

"Beginning in 1949, the pipeline took over existing routes of the old Nazi 'Rat Lines' established by Die Spinne, or the Spider, the escape arm of ODESSA, which was and is the Society for the Protection of Former SS. Today these same escape routes are again in use, assisting fleeing East German Stasi members and KGB apparatchiks no longer in favor with the current regimes.

"Another parallel is the willing participation of Western Intelligence services, for whom drugs have long been the chief means of financing covert wars and purchasing arms. The French pipeline has been dormant for decades and is easily deniable in the wake of South American and Asian drug-trafficking activity."

"Still," the cousin of the Iranian president put in, "during the initial phase of neutralization, can you coordinate the strikes with the accuracy required?"

The host smiled, his eyes twinkling in amusement. "Come to the window," he told his guests.

They turned to one another with looks of bewilderment. What could their host mean? Then the cousin of Rafsanjani shrugged and rose from his seat. He went to the window and peered outside. The others heard him gasp.

A team of commandos wearing black balaclava face masks and carrying 9 mm grease guns had tied up their bodyguards. They were lying across the hoods of their black Mercedes town cars, with the guns of the commandos pointed at the backs of their heads.

"Shall I issue the order to have them executed right now or will this demonstration be sufficient to assure you of my capabilities?" asked the host, already gleaning the answer from the ashen faces of the men in the room.

"That will not be necessary," the cousin of the president told him after a few beats, reaching for the handkerchief in his breast pocket and mopping his moisture-beaded brow. "You have adequately made your point. Apparently you have lost none of your edge."

"It is as keen as ever," the host affirmed with a nod.

"That is good," the president's cousin answered as his courage returned. "For you will need every bit of it."

He deferred to the questions of the two men who had accompanied him as guests into the villa. Then he said, "You have our full approval. Commence with your operations."

With hardly a flourish, a hard-shell attaché case was brought out. The host opened it and counted the neat bundles of hard currency stacked within. It was a down payment on his operational fee.

"Thank you," said the house owner, snapping the case shut. "You will not be disappointed with the results, I trust."

He smiled as the guests left the villa and returned to their vehicles. Going to the window, the host looked out onto the courtyard below. His commandos had vanished as quickly as they had appeared, having cut the bonds of the bodyguards with their knives before melting away.

The host watched with amusement as his departing guests shouted and gestured at their humiliated protectors before climbing into their vehicles and driving off. Then he let the curtains fall back and went to the bar to make himself a drink.

He did not know that one of those men from Tehran detested the mullahs, was still loyal to the ousted Pahlavis and was a long-time agent of the Israeli Mossad. Soon the American CIA—which shared sensitive Intelligence with Mossad, as it did with other friendly networks—would know all about the planned operations and would begin to suspect the identity of the man behind them.

PART ONE:

Shadow Warriors

1

A sniper stood in the doorway, his hand on the butt of a Heckler & Koch P7M13 semiauto augmented with a Hush Puppy-type suppressor.

Even with the suppressor, the small black firearm fit easily into the deep pocket of his stadium coat as he loitered in the shadows behind the stairs in the small vestibule.

He had selected the firearm for its compact dimensions. Despite its small size, the P7M13 would fire with stopping power to match any large-frame handgun.

Soon the shooter heard footsteps approach from the narrow street outside the vestibule door.

He had listened to the sounds made by scores of passersby during the fifteen minutes he had spent behind the stairway landing. He didn't tense until he heard the footsteps stop altogether, followed immediately by the jangle of keys as the door began to swing inward.

Viewed through the chink between the steps, the face matched the one in the photos the gunman had carefully studied. Having confirmed the target, the gunman slowly slid the P7M13 from his pocket.

With the weapon already loaded, cocked and unsafed, the target was a trigger pull away from termination. The gunman took a single short step from behind the stairwell and raised the silenced H&K.

With the muzzle bore of the suppressor less than two inches from the startled victim's face, the gunner pumped the trigger three times in quick succession.

As the target slumped to the dirty tile floor amid rolling shell casings ejected by the P7M13, the gunman was already yanking open the door.

Walking briskly through the noisy, crowded and meandering streets of Marseilles, he was soon far from the killing ground, his contract fulfilled.

SEVERAL HUNDRED MILES to the north, in Amsterdam, Holland, and only a few minutes later, another termination directive was about to be carried out.

The water bus cruised slowly along the Heerengracht Canal, one of the city's major thoroughfares for waterborne commuter traffic.

Passengers on the water bus were on their way to their jobs and not paying much attention to what was going on around them in the manner of bored commuters everywhere.

Only one passenger was outside on the observation deck, peering over the boat's guardrail through dense gray fog that had rolled in overnight.

The rest of the commuters were content to scan the morning papers within the heated comfort of the enclosed passenger compartment on the boat's upper deck.

Such was not the case with one of the passengers—a man of nondescript appearance wearing a dark blue raincoat and a soft gray felt hat—who rose from his seat in the passenger compartment and walked without looking left or right to the exit of the heated interior and stepped out onto the windy deck upon which a light drizzle was falling.

A lone man carrying a leather briefcase and smoking a cigarette was there ahead of him. The observation deck's only other occupant, he discarded his smoke, shoved one hand into his coat pocket and moved off with hardly a glance at the newcomer.

Crossing the rain-slick deck, the man in the dark blue raincoat leaned over the railing and consulted his wristwatch. Almost like clockwork, the figure appeared on the bank of the canal, visible through the sheets of swirling gray mist. He was jogging southward at a steady pace.

The man on the observation deck had been making the commuter run on the water bus during rush-hour periods for the past week, and he knew that the man always jogged this route at this hour, rain or shine, fair weather or foul.

The Ingram M-11 hung from a swivel mount beneath his dark blue raincoat. The 9 mm Cortos fired by the machine pistol were adequate. The sniper liked the compactness of the weapon and the fact that a sound suppressor could be added when required.

In less than a minute, he had attached the suppressor, pulled back the cocking lever, moved the fire-control selector from semi to full and slid back the safety.

Extending his arms, he held the machine pistol beyond the railing so that the brass would be ejected into the water instead of onto the deck of the water bus. He waited for the man in the jogging suit to reach a place where the path elbowed out and brought him within optimum range.

Then he pressed the trigger, firing off the entire contents of the 32-round staggered box magazine. At the M-11's 900 rpm cycling rate, this translated into a little under five seconds of rotoring steel and jumping brass.

When the jogger had toppled like a rag doll the shooter let the M-11 drop into the murky waters of the Heerengracht, where it promptly sank beneath the surface dimpled with the light, cold morning rain.

Seconds later the water bus had passed the place of execution where the motionless figure lay.

Termination complete, the shooter turned, confirming that he was still unobserved; he had been on deck for only a few minutes. He returned to the heated passenger compartment and took a seat close to one of the four exits, scanning the area surreptitiously to make certain that no overly curious glances were being directed his way, in which case other measures would have to be taken to prevent his description from being made known.

Satisfied that no undue notice had been taken of him, the man in the dark blue raincoat disembarked with the crowd of passengers onto the quay a few minutes later. He was soon lost amid a crop of opening umbrellas and an army of shuffling feet.

HOURS LATER, as the body of the slain jogger was discovered in Amsterdam, it was night in a rough section of Brooklyn, New York, known as Little Vietnam. An Oriental man climbed onto a bicycle and set off down the street with a brown paper bag containing a recently placed order of Chinese food.

Several minutes later, the deliveryman chained his bicycle to a parking meter and approached the front

door of an apartment building whose red brick walls
were festooned with multicolored graffiti.

Finding a door buzzer, he rang the bell and was
admitted into the cavernous lobby.

Inside the elevator, the deliveryman reached under his apron and removed a silenced Colt Mk-4
loaded with .45 ACP hollowpoint bullets. Pulling
back the slide, he cocked the weapon, chambered
the first of the clip's fifteen rounds and pulled back
the hammer.

As the elevator stopped, the deliveryman rehol-
stered the weapon beneath his apron and pushed
through the door into the tiled hallway.

The door that he wanted was directly across the
hall.

The deliveryman rang the doorbell and identified
himself at the sound of the male voice behind the
door.

It opened a moment later, and the deliveryman
stared at a middle-aged man with thinning hair in a
white T-shirt who was holding a wallet in one hand
and reaching for the brown bag of Chinese food
with the other.

As the man in the doorway took the bag, the deliveryman pulled the silenced Colt from beneath his
apron and pumped a trio of low-decibel rounds into
his chest, catapulting the man back into the foyer of
the apartment.

Entering the apartment and closing the door behind him, the deliveryman pointed the weapon at the thrashing target's head and—holding out his free hand as a blood shield—squeezed off another three rounds.

Probing swiftly through the apartment, he ascertained that he had killed the flat's sole occupant and quickly left. The recently hired deliveryman did not report back to the Szechuan take-out place that night, nor the following day. The owners could not know that he had delivered a take-out order of an entirely different sort and that he would never return again.

2

Located within the two-hundred-odd square kilometers of wooded territory that encompassed the sprawling Fort Bragg complex in North Carolina was a Special Forces training facility nicknamed the Zoo.

The secret facility contained the urban close-quarters battle range and live-fire hostage-rescue training facility, or UCQBR. The facility featured an accurate mock-up of an urban environment complete with buildings, signs and billboards of various types, parked vehicles and motorized dummies located in windows and storefronts.

The complex was manufactured by Utilex, a Hong Kong-based company, among the few firms in the world with experience at constructing combat ranges of the size and complexity of that located at the Zoo.

Building materials at the facility were constructed of a concretelike material that, unlike concrete, could absorb small-arms fire at a narrow angle without allowing the bullet to ricochet.

Overseeing the close-quarters battle range was a protected control tower from which it was possible to cause the dummies to move about, grenades to detonate, weapons to fire along fixed lines of sight and to simulate other aspects of an urban combat environment.

All of these effects were intended to stress the combat reflexes of Special Forces personnel to the maximum possible limits.

Closed circuit TV cameras monitored every inch of the facility, transmitting real-time video to the control tower where supervisory personnel could oversee and control every phase of activity.

The idea behind the UCQBR was to provide trainees with field exercises that replicate real-world situations as closely as possible.

From ducking and answering retaliatory fire to dealing with simulated hostage situations, field assets undergoing training at the UCQBR complex were given the opportunity to learn and make mistakes in an environment where errors weren't fatal.

The scenario that SLAM—or search, locate, annihilate mission team—was working on during the team's period of UCQBR simulator qualification time was based on a hypothetical terrorist grab of friendlies encountered during the course of an anti-narcotic operation.

The object of the sophisticated war game was to prepare the SLAM strike team for the eventuality of a planned counternarcotic interdiction raid turning into an unexpected hostage situation.

It was also an opportunity for Deal Slater, Mason Hawke and Eddie Bishop to get a hands-on feel for the new H&K MP/5-10 SMGs they had just been issued as part of their field kit. Slater had pushed for the new high-tech SMGs and was gratified to get his pick of the first weapons consignment coming into Bragg from the H&K plant in Germany.

Almost identical in size and weight to the MP-5 submachine guns familiar to special-forces members across the globe, the MP/5-10 SMG fired heavier and more powerful 10 mm rounds and had an expanded magazine capacity of sixty-five rounds.

The three SLAM commandos were about to put those weapons to the test as Slater and Bishop checked the pull capacity of the climbing ropes secured to their waist at one end and grapnels on the rooftop at the other.

Wearing standard NATO-pattern camo BDUs, their combat dress included black United Body Armor Equipment TAC-100R tactical face masks and flak vests, both constructed of Kevlar and both capable of stopping rounds from most handguns, shotguns and subguns even at close range. The flak vests protected their vital areas beneath their camo field jackets.

Black fingerless tactical gloves protected hands while leaving fingers free to manipulate the triggers, safeties and fire-select studs of the H&K SMGs slung across their backs.

Sporting an M-16A2 autorifle, Mason Hawke was positioned in the narrow corridor just outside the flat in which the hostage condition prevailed and one story below the building rooftop on which his two partners stood.

"Three. We're in position and proceeding to move," Slater said into the microphone attached to the comset in the "prick" pouch on his load bearings.

"Affirm on that," Hawke replied, steadying the short-barreled M-16A2 assault weapon and keeping his eyes glued on the locked door of the flat. "I'm good to go."

"We copy, over."

A moment later Slater nodded to Bishop and both unconventional-warfare specialists began to speed rappel down opposite walls of the building, paying out the rope with expert precision as they descended from the roof in a speed measured in heartbeats.

Quickly they reached their targets: windows set one story down from the roof.

The three-way play that went down next happened with blinding speed and lethal efficiency.

Faces protected by tactical masks, Slater and Bishop crashed through the glass panes to target their MP/5-10 on the heads of two terrorist mannequins and take out each one in the "tap-tap" style perfected by the SAS—two shots directed either at the head or to the chest—a style that had become the training norm for worldwide counterterror forces from Germany's GSG-9 to America's own Delta.

While this was happening, Hawke kicked in the door to the flat and went steamrollering into the room on a half crouch. He was already cutting loose with a quick burst of 5.56 mm steeljacketed lead as he broke sideways to take out the other two terrorist mannequins inside the room.

Like Slater and Bishop, he had taken down his targets without harming a single hair on a friendly's head.

"Not bad," Slater said, checking his Tag-Huer wrist chronometer after hitting the stopwatch function. The entire strike had taken less than four minutes. "But it could be a lot smoother. Let's take five, then run through it one more time."

JACK CALLIXTO faced the small camera on his desk phone. He was about to place a videophone network call to Slater, Hawke and Bishop from his Washington, D.C., office.

The line was secure, but how secure was any telephone line, encrypted or otherwise?

The orders had filtered down the chain of command by the usual circuitous route, one not amenable to tracing, at least not easily or without knowing certain highly classified names and numbers.

The orders had come as a result of the warning recently received via brush contact in Iran. The message had been from one of the Iranians who had been party to a reported clandestine meeting at a villa in Tehran during which plans had been made for a series of execution-style hits that were to take place across the globe.

The brush contact had subsequently led to an Intelligence assessment but to no immediate action. Not until the murders across the globe had started, that is. Only then did the bureaucratic wheels begin to finally turn.

The unifying thread between all the hits was the linkage between the deceased parties and the old French Connection heroin pipeline.

Each had been a principal in the Istanbul-Marseilles drug conduit from its heyday in the late 1960s on up to a far reduced role in the dwindling international drug trade of the eighties and nineties.

As more Intelligence began pouring into the loop, it became clear that what was now taking place was nothing less than a purge of the old guard and its replacement by a new infrastructure bent on taking over the turf. The names and numbers that made up that infrastructure were not yet known, but analysts had detected a variety of disturbing indicators.

First were reports of increased drug-trafficking activity along the Iran-Afghanistan border.

In the wake of the gulf war and the return of American hostages kidnapped in Lebanon had come a declaration by the Iranian theocracy that the Islamic republic would pursue a grand strategy of imperial designs with its aim being the establishment of an Islamic empire encompassing Afghanistan and the newly liberated Soviet Muslim republics.

Hezbollah—the terror organization that was in reality an arm of the Iranian Mukhabarat or Intelligence service, Sawama—prepared for and carried out a renewed terror campaign.

At the same time new liaisons with the Afghan *mujahedeen* were made, which built a heroin pipeline down from the rebel units strung out across the hill country into neighboring Iran.

Second, throughout the territory of the former Soviet Union, Iranian, Libyan and Iraqi agents were combing the landscape in a feverish hunt for technology experts willing to trade their expertise for money and better living conditions.

Intelligence described the primary search to be principally centered on locating and co-opting those with expertise in the construction of nuclear weapons.

As a result of such overtures, several former Soviet weapons experts were now working in Middle Eastern dictatorships on the production of fissionable materials of nuclear-weapon grade.

It had become apparent that there was a strong link between the increased flow of drugs and the search for nuclear-weapons expertise.

In light of the stated objectives of Iran, Libya and Iraq to acquire such sophisticated weapons technology, it was apparent that a new pipeline to sell drugs and raise cash was being established.

Deal Slater and his men were about to be charged by Jack Callixto with dismantling that pipeline, piece by piece, if necessary. With full presidential approval, stopping the flow of drugs at its source would be SLAM's next mission priority.

3

Slater, Hawke and Bishop deployed into the operations zone on three separate flights, each of which originated from a different departure point in the United States or in Europe.

All SLAM personnel reached Marseilles International Airport within a few hours of each other.

The three covert-warfare specialists were checked through customs without incident bearing flash I.D. supplied by SLAM's Intelligence support activity, code-named Yellow Light.

But in the case of team commander Deal Slater, not all went smoothly.

While Hawke and Bishop passed through customs undetected, a sharp-eyed airport security agent who was monitoring the arrivals on a closed circuit monitor had identified the new arrival as someone of whom to take special note.

All governments compiled "watch lists" of those who, for various political and operational reasons, were deemed of importance and bore close scrutiny. Deal Slater, due to his covert activities throughout the years, was one of these aforementioned individuals.

The security man at the airport recognized the face beneath the soft felt hat and punched up a still from the videotape feed coming off the closed circuit TV cameras. A computer check turned up a close similarity to Slater, one that was close enough for the security agent to read as a confirm.

But the confirm was never reported.

Not to the arm of the French Ministry of Defense, the Groupe d'Intervention de la Gendarmerie Nationale—GIGN—which was responsible for that nation's counterterror activities and internal-security arrangements.

The security agent, a native of Algeria, was secretly working for the Libyan Mukhabarat and he had recently received instructions from his case officer to attach priority importance to sightings of any known U.S. Intelligence personnel passing through his surveillance station. This he did at a dead drop during a lunch break only an hour after the sighting.

On arrival via diplomatic pouch a little while later, the raw Intelligence was analyzed in Tripoli.

Soon the finished Intelligence product was being passed to the Iranians and the fattish man with the Spanish accent ensconced in the villa in Tehran, who dispatched a hit team to France comprised of members of Hezbollah, the Iranian Party of God.

FINAL PREPARATIONS WERE being made to bring the Hezbollah shooters into France, a process that would involve circuitous travel arrangements since the French GIGN would move swiftly against such men if sighted. In the meantime the SLAM team had arrived separately at a CIA safehouse in the St. Antoine district.

Mason Hawke, SLAM's technical and communications officer, was gratified to find that the Intelsat down-link equipment was in good order and functioned correctly.

He immediately sat at the console and began punching in coded sequences that would put him in touch with a KH-12 phased satellite array located approximately fifty kilometers above the earth in a low orbit.

While Hawke sat at the computer equipment, Slater and Bishop inspected the military ordnance requisitioned for the strike. The equipment manifest tallied with the hardware on-site.

Three carrying cases with Heckler-Koch MP/5-10 submachine guns nestled in their die-cut foam interiors were waiting for the team, as were several hundred rounds of 10 mm ammo for the guns and spare ABS plastic magazines. The ammunition came in two forms: green tracers and standard full-metal-jacketed hardball.

Hush Puppy-type silencers, which were custom threaded for each weapon by CIA armor artificers, were also included in the package to afford SLAM with the capability to inflict whispering death on the opposition.

The SLAM team chose the H&Ks above the Colt Commando SMGs for two main reasons.

First, there were special field requirements, dictated by the trade-off between firepower and concealability, for which the H&K SMG appeared to be the best choice hands down.

Second, the mission parameters would call for close-quarters fighting, for which the MP/5-10 SMGs had a small but decisive tactical edge.

But as far as personal sidearms went, the SIG-Sauer P-228 9 mm semiautomatic pistols favored by SLAM would continue to be standard armament on this current search-and-destroy run.

The compact SIGs—outfitted with the currently fashionable New York trigger—were concealable, controllable and had the stopping power of large-frame handguns.

Battle dress for the mission included NATO-standard camouflage BDUs, Kevlar tactical vests, tactical face masks and load-bearing suspenders.

The load bearings were equipped with mag and radio pouches for the compact AN/PCR-3000 communicator units, which were equipped with constrictor straps. The UM84 Universal Military Holster for the P-228s also hung from the suspenders. Miscellaneous items provided for SLAM included Cyalume light-sticks, climbing tackle, APERS, frag and stun grenades, and the battletested Ka-bar combat knives preferred by each member of the SLAM team above more modern designs due to their proven reliability and feel in the hand.

Having carefully gone over the equipment manifest, Slater and Bishop turned to Mason Hawke. Seated at a console bearing several high-definition computer screens he had patched into the KH-12 satellite array and was now receiving telemetry directly from the spy satellite's orbital perspective.

This encoded transmission was converted into a real-time high-resolution graphic display by the sophisticated image-processing architecture of the proprietary computer hardware.

The system deployed had been custom-designed by Seymour Cray specifically for use in the field. It was rumored that Cray had devoted so much attention toward making the system state-of-the-art that the Cray computer company had delayed a supercomputer delivery to the Lawrence Livermore Laboratories, a thirty-million-dollar loss that had been made up by the CIA out of covert imprest funds.

The twenty-four-inch noninterlaced VGA screen to which Slater and Bishop devoted their attention was a top-down view of one of the islands lying just off the coast of Marseilles. A sidebar identified this particular spit of land in the Mediterranean as Chat Noir—Black Cat.

"Note the fortifications," Hawke said to Slater and Bishop, highlighting the terrain feature he was pointing out with a cursor in the shape of an arrow. "These cylindrical structures here in the upper left are gun emplacements. I make them as Norinco Type-75 or 75-1, 14.5 mm triple-A guns."

"Looks like troop barracks, too," Slater put in, noting a series of oblong features over to the right of the satellite photo.

"Good guess," Hawke put in. "That's probably right."

Before the Keyhole satellite passed over the target, Hawke had pointed out a number of other features on the island, both natural and man-made, that would prove either useful or detrimental to an assault force. All would be taken into account during the final planning phase of the mission.

Black Cat Island housed one of the largest heroin refining plants in the world. It was to be SLAM's target on the Marseilles strike.

4

Slater and the two other members of the SLAM strike team prepared to converge on the target zone at 0349 hours Zulu or Greenwich meantime.

They were outfitted with camouflage BDUs from which ordnance and other combat matériel were festooned on load-bearing suspenders. Their combat dress included the milspec "Fritz" helmets optionally equipped with ghillie cover, and tactical face masks were also part of the field kit.

Equipment to be utilized on the strike included small-footprint communications apparatus.

As on previous operations, AN/PRC-3000 comsets were carried high on each SLAM member's chest in radio pouches, thereby placing the "pricks" within easy reach.

The H&K MP/5-10 SMGs with which SLAM had gained proficiency at the Zoo now rode their backs on TEAM slings as SLAM prepared to deploy.

Their target was a fortified villa that lay beyond the heights of the island's coast. The sprawling estate had been defensively fortified, and new structures and earthworks had been added to the compound in support of the illicit narcotics-processing activities conducted thereon.

About thirty meters beyond the wave-tossed beach of the southern French coastline to which they had deployed, the SLAM team spotted the infrared strobe that marked the position of the trawling vessel that they had been expecting.

Invisible to the naked eye, the IR strobe was readily discernible to SLAM thanks to the AN/PVS night-vision goggles they wore.

The commandos replied with a signal strobe of their own and deployed to the beach zone.

Once the skipper of the vessel exchanged verbal recognition codes with Slater and his men—who kept their weapons trained on him until he had done so, a necessity dictated by proper fieldcraft procedures—they boarded the boat. Despite its ramshackle appearance, the boat was powered by a thousand-horsepower Mercruiser engine.

The skipper was a CIA contract operative who came from a long line of those doing jobs for the Company in furtherance of their political beliefs. His father had been a member of a French partisan network who during World War II had assisted the legendary Jedburg teams of the OSS and had himself participated in several covert ops during the Cold War years.

The boat was equipped with a few other nonstandard high-tech features, including sophisticated radar and sonar gear and long range, satellite-capable communications equipment.

But the most surprising nonstandard feature of the vessel was the cargo that it carried concealed under a tarp on its afterdeck. This was a versatile craft known as a subskimmer.

The subskimmer was developed by the British for use by the SBS, or Special Boat Services, the equivalent of the U.S. Navy's famous SEALs. Designed to carry out waterborne commando assault-style missions, the rigid-hull inflatable craft was powered by its ninety-horsepower outboard engine when it was a surface vessel. As a stealthy submersible, it was powered when fully submerged by two battery-enabled electric motors.

The skipper of the trawling vessel knew what was expected of him. He was to bring the boat out to within a kilometer of the Chat Noir shoreline, then drop anchor.

While the subskimmers were capable of shuttling SLAM the entire distance from shore, it was deemed advisable from a tactical standpoint to have the takedown specialists deploy from the ocean under cover of darkness.

The American commandos on board would then proceed the rest of the way underwater, meeting up with the boat on completion of the mission.

While the trawler chugged through the moonless night, Slater, Hawke and Bishop occupied themselves by climbing into their wet suits and strapping the supplied CCR-25 closed circuit oxygen scuba apparatus onto their backs.

Designed for long-duration shallow-depth military diving, the CCR-25 rebreathers functioned by scrubbing carbon dioxide from recycled air through advanced-design chemical filters and did not leave behind a trail of bubbles as was the case with conventional scuba tanks.

Permitting dives up to three hours in duration, the units were well suited to facilitate stealthy incursion activities in pursuit of covert-strike objectives.

The skipper told Slater and company that the boat was in position just over a half kilometer beyond the island in the dark seas, and assisted them in lowering the subskimmer over the side of the vessel using a cable winch.

As the delivery craft was being lowered, the subskimmer's front flotation bladder was pumped full of compressed air to keep the bow from dipping and to stabilize the craft. Once the vessel was in the water, the three SLAM commandos went over the side of the boat and seated themselves inside the sub-skimmer.

The skipper of the vessel watched the covert delivery craft submerge as the front bladder was deflated and its buoyancy box was partially voided to establish a negative buoyancy. The three men vanished from sight beneath the surface of the ink black waters.

Moments later there was not a single trace of the commando team. With a brief glance at the dark hulk of Black Cat Island in the near distance, the skipper turned and went back into the wheelhouse.

His role in the mission complete, at least for the present, he raised anchor and began to chug from the drop zone.

5

With Eddie Bishop behind the handlebar controls, the subskimmer glided beneath the waters of the Mediterranean like some hydra-headed sea beast.

Its specially silenced engine and the rebreather gear SLAM wore all combined to make the commando raider unit's progress utterly stealthy.

In a short while the SLAM strike specialists, navigating by means of submersible underwater night-vision goggles that incorporated an infrared source for improved visibility under poor ambient-light conditions, had negotiated the marine environment and had reached the vicinity of Black Cat Island.

They had already scouted out a protected hiding place for the subskimmer by carefully analyzing the high-grade satellite visuals that had been beamed down from the KH-12 spy platforms in low-trajectory earth orbit.

The hide site selected was a small marine cove from which the beach zone could be quickly ac-

quired by climbing a gently sloping though rocky
rise. Still keeping the subskimmer submerged,
Bishop jockeyed the nimble little craft into the cove,
then forced air into its buoyancy box from the amphibious unit's compressed-air tanks.

The subskimmer broke the surface of the water
like a many-headed sea creature rising in the night
as its flotation bladders filled with compressed
air.

Tying it fast by hawser lines to nearby rocks, the
three strikers removed their scuba gear and, garbed
in the camo BDUs they had worn underneath their
suits, waded in the shallow water toward the rocky
beach.

While Slater and Hawke kept guard, scanning the
shoreline through standard NVGs and keeping the
H&K MP/5-10 SMGs ready to engage hostiles
should any appear, Bishop took the point, making
for the heights. Signaling the all-clear, Bishop saw
Slater and Hawke make to follow him through the
green electronic viewfield of his NVGs.

Within a matter of seconds all three SLAM strikers were in place on the ground. They were now deployed in depth to perform their preliminary
reconnaissance of the strike perimeter.

Three specters stole across the windswept landscape, seeing the strike zone through their flickering electronic eyes.

The aggressor team was on-site and mobile.

SLAM owned the night.

SLATER, HAWKE AND BISHOP stealthily moved to preplanned strike sectors on the perimeter of the drug refinement plant. The sectors were code-named Amber, Blue and Chrome, respectively.

Keeping low and trusting that the pattern-breaking properties of their BDUs' NATO camo pattern would render them invisible in the indigo blackness, each member of the SLAM team scanned his individual sector through AN/PVS third-generation night-vision goggles.

From his position of concealment behind a jumble of black basaltic, Deal Slater kept his MP/5-10 in front of him as he lay doggo and swept his glance back and forth in a practiced scanning pattern.

His sector appeared to be in much the state of readiness that he had expected.

There was one guard walking his perimeter. The sentry was not equipped with NVGs and carried an FN/FAL long-barreled rifle variant, a common firearm in that part of the world, more so than the ubiquitous Kalashnikov Avtomats and their numerous derivatives.

While Slater continued his prestrike sector scan, Mason Hawke was performing similar recon operations on his end of the mission.

The shimmering green video viewfield of Hawke's NVGs revealed that his own sector was ripe for a strike.

Eddie Bishop was in position, as well, as he trained the Pilkington-Pound image-intensification scope of his MP/5-10 on the sentry in the guard tower overhead, having pushed his NVGs up on his head.

The security crow's nest was some thirty meters in height. When the sentry within its confines was perfectly framed between the white cross reticles of the starlight scope, Bishop took a deep breath and squeezed off a sound-suppressed 9 mm round.

He watched the asset in the crow's nest as he was pitched backward by the impact of the single round that penetrated the left quadrant of his torso and punctured his heart. A spray of blood marked the single entrance wound.

A moment later Deal Slater heard the three radio clicks signaling that Bishop in position at Chrome had taken out the opposition resource in the crow's nest and was deploying into the target strike perimeter. Slater heard the two answering clicks that signaled that Hawke was moving on Blue.

Deal Slater reached toward the AN/PCR-3000 nestled in its Velcro pouch on the load-bearing suspenders he wore and depressed the comset's talk button once, sending his own confirmation to Hawke and Bishop. Then, his weapon held at the ready, he broke from his position toward Amber, negotiating the windswept ground at a low, fast trot.

6

Two 10 mm bursts from the MP/5-10 in Deal Slater's gloved hands dropped the sentry in his tracks.

Wearing khaki fatigues, the perimeter walker had been on patrol when Slater had jumped from the top of the fence behind him.

The opposition player had spun around at the sound and brought up his weapon.

Slater had already acquired his man with the MP/5-10. In such a tactical situation it was the combatant who "got the drop" on his opponent.

The sound-suppressed bursts exited the subgun's Hush Puppy-type muzzle with barely a whisper, punching through the sentry's heart, inducing large amounts of blood.

The man dropped to the dirt, and Slater dragged him quickly from sight, concealing him in the shadowy recesses just within the perimeter enclosure.

Precision coordinated with Slater's lethal actions, Bishop and Hawke were taking down their targets at Blue and Chrome sectors.

The targets were terminated swiftly and silently, and these were also stashed where they were likely to remain undiscovered for some time to come.

Having dispatched their designated targets, Slater, Bishop and Hawke proceeded to the second assigned phase of the base penetration.

During this phase, each member of the team would go to his preselected demolition site and place timed high-explosive munitions packages containing the high-blast-yield compound, Octol. Then the strike force would leave the target area one by one and withdraw to the rally point on the beach zone.

SLATER'S ASSIGNED demolition site was the heroin refinery. Reaching this priority target by loping stealthily through the shadows, he wasn't surprised by signs of activity at the site, a low-rise building of cinder block with a slab roof.

As he covertly scanned the combat environment through NVGs, a four-by that had entered through the villa's main gates pulled up and three men got out.

These individuals promptly vanished inside the refinery area. Slater thought he recognized Hans Rohlfing and Chivu Mihalescu, two key assets Intel had linked to the drug activities on Chat Noir.

Slater waited until they were out of sight and unshipped the munitions he'd brought along.

Removing the circular black general-purpose mines, each containing six kilograms of Octol-based plastic explosive, Slater slotted the demo charges at critical points along the exterior of the building. They were placed so that the force of the blast would hurl the walls inward when detonated, resulting in maximum structural damage.

Although the charges were enabled with radio-linked backup, it was possible to detonate them manually should operational contingencies require it. However, a timed explosion was the favored method of ignition.

Slater inserted a detonator into each mine, then set the timers for a twelve-minute delay. He moved quickly toward his preassigned extraction point.

By this point Bishop and Hawke were completing their tasks, as well. Bishop was taking longer due to the necessity of terminating the sentry guarding the base arms depot.

Shooting the sentry at close range, Bishop quickly neutralized the lock on the steel door using a torque hammer device and was soon inside. The charges slotted, he was out again in just under six minutes.

Hawke's assigned demolition site was the barracks buildings housing the refinery's rank-and-file personnel.

He had drawn this assignment principally because he was practiced at taking these structures down. He was also adept at crawling under, around and through populated areas without being detected.

Sliding into the crawl space between the cool dirt and the floor of the building, Hawke slotted his demo charges, hearing the sounds of footfalls over his head. Having completed his tasks, he moved stealthily through the darkness of the compound toward his assigned extraction point, alternating fast sprints with sudden halts to scan for countersurveillance activity.

In a matter of minutes the three SLAM strikers had come and gone like shadows in the night. Unseen and unknown, they had primed the base for one hell of an explosion.

SLATER HAD already reached his extraction point and was tugging on the nylon rope that was anchored to the top of the wall by a steel grapnel.

Reaching the rally point Slater consulted his wrist chronometer and pressed the stud that illuminated the dial with infrared light readily visible through his night goggles. The line of digits informed Slater that it was just over three minutes to detonation. Bishop and Hawke had better hustle.

About a minute later his two colleagues rejoined him at rally point Donkey. They hunkered behind the protection of the jumble of basaltic boulders just above the cove where the subskimmer was moored. Slater, consulting his chronometer, unshipped the remote fire-control unit to be used just in case the timers did not trigger the munitions.

Like Slater, Hawke and Bishop removed their night-vision goggles, blinking away the lingering afterimages, which usually required several minutes to fade completely.

The countdown toward detonation continued until only a line of zeros remained on the face of Slater's watch. A pulse beat later Slater realized that the remote backup would not be necessary. A blinding white incandescence lit up the horizon, exposing the terrain that had been hidden under cover of darkness.

Despite the advanced antibloom features of their night-vision goggles, the team would have been blinded by the light of the blast had they been wearing their image intensification goggles.

The thunderclap of the primary charges exploding in perfect synchronization came a fraction of a second later, traveling far slower than the light generated by the blast but faster than the concussive wave front that arrived a second after the sound of the explosion.

As they watched the entire base go up in a ballooning mass of hellfire, Slater, Hawke and Bishop felt the searing heat and blast effect finally reach them. With Bishop in the lead, they turned and scrambled down the incline toward the cove, Slater at the rear of the three-man column covering their retreat.

After boarding the subskimmer, the three covert commandos once again donned their scuba suits.

While Slater and Hawke pushed the subskimmer into open water, Bishop was putting the delivery craft into a dive.

Once fully submerged, SLAM proceeded underwater until they detected the flash of the infrared strobe from the trawler. The skipper helped them aboard. They watched the last fires of the destroyed base on Black Cat Island as he set course for the mainland and pulled out the throttle for the short trip back.

7

The shooter team dispatched by Hezbollah had missed the American commandos who had been its targets in the south of France.

As it had turned out, the terrorists had arrived mere hours after the SLAM strikers had left the country in the wake of a devastating assault on a major illicit drug-processing facility.

Millions of dollars had been poured into the ultramodern heroin factory so far, and the damage inflicted on the property was exceeded in scope only by the damage to key personnel inflicted by the precision-timed exploitation strike.

Among those who burned to death in the strike were Hans Rohlfing and Chivu Mihalescu, the former one of the best chemists in the business, the latter a former Romanian Securitate section chief who was a genius at transportation and logistics.

These two losses meant that the estimated thousand tons of high-grade heroin that the plant had been scheduled to turn out over time would be lost, and the means of transporting the valuable product overseas to lucrative American markets had also been destroyed.

The Hezbollah group—dubbed Ishtar by the fat-faced man in the villa in Iran who was heading the mission—had no choice but to redeploy to Brussels and initiate a search for their targets.

Their controller—the man in Iran with the Spanish accent—was taking full responsibility for the debacle that had occurred. He could not afford to let his Iranian patrons down. They would not easily forgive and forget. They could be just as ruthless as his ever-watchful and highly dangerous enemies to whom he owed blood chit. They lived by a different and far more ancient creed that demanded an eye for an eye.

Then again, so did he. Next time, he vowed, the outcome would be different.

ANOTHER MAJOR SETBACK occurred with the destruction of a heroin-storage depot in the rough Marolles section of Brussels.

Like its counterpart on Black Cat Island, the warehouse had become the target of a devastating and mysterious bombing strike, carried out with commando-style precision.

Had the horse stored at the depot not been largely removed the previous day, the Iranians would have taken decisive and brutal steps, turning on their leader savagely.

But the cargo was already on its way to transshipment points in Europe, so it would not so easily be interdicted. Fate had granted the man in the villa in Tehran a second chance.

He was determined not to risk failure a third time.

DEAL SLATER, Mason Hawke and Eddie Bishop left Belgian territory via two separate routes from Brussels.

The strike against the heroin depot had had mixed results, since post-op Intelligence revealed that most of the dope had already been removed from the storehouse before the hit.

Still, the depot itself was gone, and the opposition would be hard-pressed to find another adequate stash site. Escape was now the team's primary objective.

Eddie Bishop took a fast TGV train from Brussels to Paris, where he could connect with a direct flight to Washington. Slater and Hawke would drive to Ostend over the EEC's excellent road system, catch the ferry there, and leave Europe via the U.K. All three carried weapons.

Since SLAM had begun operations, the strike team had been refining its techniques, honing them to a razor edge of combat readiness.

Each mission brought new insights into the way the team operated. Post-operational analysis gave Slater and his crew the chance to fine-tune their tactics to meet forthcoming threats.

What had happened to the team in Thailand during operations against heroin lord Kuhn Sa was one of those situations which lent itself to a doctrinal about-face.

Prior to Thailand, SLAM's procedural doctrine called for extraction from op zones with minimal weaponry. But Bishop and Hawke had wound up nearly paying with their lives at Don Muang International Airport when they had encountered a hit crew wielding 7.62 mm automatic rifles while they were armed only with the 9 mm SIG P-228 pistols.

The SIGs were fine weapons. But they had the limitations inherent in any single-shot weapon firing the Luger or parabellum round when up against long-barreled or repeating weapons cycling out heavier caliber bullets with higher terminal ballistic qualities.

Bishop and Hawke had been hazardously outgunned at Don Muang and had nearly lost their lives. Slater, equipped with his Beretta 93-R machine pistol, had fared far better against similarly armed assailants.

It became apparent in post-operational analysis that the burst-fire capability and higher magazine capacity of the Beretta had made a significant difference and given Slater the critical edge.

As a result of this after-battle assessment, SLAM changed its operational doctrine to include the carrying of compact, concealable automatic weapons on extraction.

After trial and error at the Zoo's training center at Bragg, where SLAM worked out between missions, Bishop and Hawke had settled upon the Ingram M-11 as their weapon of choice. Not much larger than the longtime GI-issue M1911 semiautomatic pistol, the M-11s were chambered for the 9 mm short round.

Back home at the Zoo's firing range, the SLAM personnel had become proficient in using the deadly weapon. As far as Deal Slater was concerned, though, the full-auto-capable Beretta 93-R had worked fine before and would function well again.

As he and Mason Hawke drove their rental car toward the ferryboat that was soon to depart Ostend for the British mainland, Slater's 93-R was tucked away in his shoulder rig while Hawke wore the M-11 beneath his Windbreaker.

It turned out to be fortunate for both men, as it would be for Bishop, too, that they had taken the precaution of leaving Brussels armed.

8

Eddie Bishop was engrossed in reading the *International Herald Tribune.* The lead story concerned a recent outbreak of ethnic violence in the Ukraine, but significant editorial space was devoted to a report of special interest to him. "A highly placed source" in the French Ministry of Defense claimed that the recent bombing of "a handbag factory" on Black Cat Island, and another bombing of "a textile warehouse" in Brussels, were not the work of terrorists as had been first claimed but part of a secret campaign by the United States government to interdict drug traffickers.

The article included a denial by the U.S. President of any such clandestine paramilitary operations in support of American antidrug policy, as well as subsequent assurances by various European heads of state that they would investigate the reports of such activity in their own countries.

Bishop was turning the page when he became aware of a striking sight. Her face was framed in straight blond hair and dominated by a pair of ice-blue eyes, full lips and those high bones that models have.

Bishop smiled in embarrassment and received an ambiguous look in exchange. He went back to reading his paper, although his mind was no longer on the article in front of him.

After a light lunch in the train's dining car, Bishop found a spot at the small, crowded bar and ordered a Scotch on the rocks, knowing that the bourbon wouldn't be any good on a European train. As he sipped his drink, he caught a flash of blond hair from the interior of the car and turned to glimpse the same woman he'd seen earlier in the passenger car. This time she held his eyes long enough for Bishop to read more meaning into the glance.

"Ask the lady what she would like to drink, please," Bishop told the bartender. "And ask her if I might join her."

"Oui, monsieur," the bartender said with a smile. He soon returned. "The lady has requested a martini and would not mind your joining her. Your drink, sir?"

Bishop told the bartender to bring him another of the same as he made for the woman's table across the packed bar car.

She smiled as he approached and met his eyes with a look of frank appraisal, and Bishop was momentarily uncomfortable as he realized that she was checking him out the way men usually did with women.

He wondered as he slid into the chair if she was rating him between one and ten. Times had certainly changed since he'd gone to high school.

It did not occur to Bishop that her appraising glance was directed at the barely discernible bulge beneath the left armpit of his loosely cut jacket where the M-11 was nestled in his shoulder harness. For the moment he had thoughts of a different sort as the drinks arrived.

"I don't want you to think I'm usually this forward," he told the woman, who had introduced herself as Olivia Chadwick, then stated her nationality as British, her occupation as chemical engineer and her destination as Paris.

"Surely, you're not," she told him, sipping her drink. Her eyes told Bishop she meant otherwise.

"Actually I'm the shy retiring type," he went on, having indentified himself as John Franklin, security consultant. "And frankly, you're too beautiful for me not to try to meet you."

She laughed, tossed back her hair and responded, "Not six hours ago I slapped the face of a leering Italian film producer who said very much the same to me. But in your case I'll accept the remark as a compliment."

"Why?" asked Bishop, noticing out of the corner of his eye that two men at a nearby table seemed to be staring at them with special interest.

"For two reasons," she replied. "The first is that you are one heck of a lot better looking than the Italian film producer. The second is that unlike him, I believe you're sincere."

"Now I think you may be handing me a line," Bishop returned, signaling the waiter. They talked over dinner and had a few more rounds, after which Olivia stretched and told Bishop it was getting late. "I'll walk you back to your compartment," he offered, and she accepted. It turned out that Bishop's compartment was at the opposite end of the same car.

"Well, good night," she told him. "Thanks for the drinks."

"My pleasure," Bishop said. As she went inside, he asked, "Maybe I'll see you tomorrow?"

"Why not? We'll still be on the same train, won't we?" Olivia responded, and Bishop heard the sound of the snap lock of the compartment door engage.

As he turned toward his own compartment, he caught a glimpse of what seemed to be the two men he'd suspected of watching him in the bar car. But when he went to investigate, nobody was there.

THE CAR FERRY between Ostend and the English mainland pulled out of its slip, leaving behind a frothing wake generated by its rapidly turning screws. The weather was cold with just a hint of drizzle, and the sun had been playing tag with the clouds all day.

On board amid dozens of passengers were Deal Slater and Mason Hawke, who planned to retrieve their rented Mercedes sedan at the other end and drive to Heathrow Airport outside London for their flight back stateside.

Also on board were three passengers who had followed the Mercedes from Brussels to Ostend. Terrorists dispatched by Hezbollah, their objective was to prevent the two American commandos from ever reaching the other side of the North Sea.

9

Professional paranoia manifested itself after Bishop had returned to his sleeper compartment on board the TGV express.

He'd begun by replaying his dinner with the charming Olivia with a smile but had soon considered other possibilities as the mental videotape automatically freeze-framed in a few key spots.

Bishop focused on two points in particular. The first was the way she had looked at him when he'd come over to her table. Had she been scanning him for a weapon?

The second point concerned the two men. The first man had a linebacker's build and close-cropped blond hair, and his movements were quick and almost surgically precise. The other man was dark and wiry with longish hair and heavy-lidded eyes. He'd been seated at an adjoining table, watching Bishop from a distance.

Bishop had decided to keep the M-11 close at hand in the event that his fears turned out to be justified. Once he might have shrugged off the nagging suspicions in his mind, but Thailand had made a believer out of Eddie Bishop.

Lulled by the rhythmic clickety-clack sound of the train as it trundled over the railway tracks and the good Scotch whiskey he'd drunk earlier, Bishop was adrift in a twilight state as he heard the repeated raps on the door of his sleeper compartment.

"Who is it?" he asked, the Ingram gripped in his hands with a round nestled in its firing chamber and its cocking lever retracted.

"It's Olivia," the voice came from the corridor. "I got kind of lonely in my compartment, and I thought you might want some company."

Bishop reminded himself that it was only in spy movies that the beautiful femme fatale wove a tender trap for her male victims.

On the other hand, truth imitated fiction often enough. In Bishop's line of work he could not afford to overlook the maxim stating that just because you happen to be paranoid does not mean they're not out to get you.

Bishop opened the door and dragged Olivia rudely inside, pressing a gun muzzle against her head and a silencing hand across her mouth.

She was further subjected to a brief and thorough frisk by the interesting man she had come to visit, a search that turned up nothing of any danger to Bishop but which did cause him considerable embarrassment.

"Look, I'm sorry," he told her afterward, staring into her wild, fear-tinged eyes. He safed the Ingram and slid it under the Murphy bed. "If you want to call the porter, go ahead. If you want to slap me, go ahead, too. I deserve it for the way I just treated you."

"An explanation will do nicely," she told him frostily.

"As I told you, I'm in the security business," Bishop went on, reciting his legend. "I have enemies. I was afraid that maybe— "

"That I was setting you up?" she asked. "You are quite a fellow, Mr. Franklin, if that is really your name."

He heard the anger drain out of Olivia's voice and saw her smile in the semidarkness. "Whoever you are," she went on, "I accept your apology and would like to give you what I originally intended."

"What was that?" Bishop asked.

"This, Mr. Franklin," she told him, shrugging off her robe and letting it fall to the floor. She put her arms around his bare waist and pressed her breasts against his chest while her lips searched out his own.

THE CORRIDOR WAS STILL as Bishop, a much happier man, unlatched the compartment door to go to the washroom at the other end of the car.

"Keep it locked until I knock like this," he said. He demonstrated on the woodwork, then pulled on his jeans and placed the Ingram in the garrison belt, pulling on an epaulette shirt over the weapon.

Her eyes had been on the gun the entire time.

"You know, Mr. Franklin," she told Bishop, lying in the bunk naked from the waist up, "I do believe you really *are* serious."

"Better believe it," Bishop told the woman as he left the compartment and walked down the empty corridor, its silence broken only by the steady clickety-clack of the train's wheels.

A few minutes later, as Bishop was emerging from the washroom, he witnessed a sight that both horrified and angered him: the big crew-cut blond and the wiry dark guy were standing outside his compartment and the door was opening as Olivia unlatched the bolt, apparently heedless of her lover's warning.

Time moved slowly as Bishop brought the Ingram into play, but even as he extended the M-11 SMG in a two-handed match grip and aimed it at his quarry he knew it was too late.

The big guy had already dragged the screaming, naked woman out of the compartment and was pressing the muzzle of a pistol against her head. His wiry partner, meanwhile, was stepping toward Bishop, jerking the barrel of the pistol, which was aimed at Bishop, while shouting for him to drop the Ingram.

Although he knew it would probably result in a bullet for both himself and Olivia, Bishop was about to let go of the autoweapon. But then, without warning, the porter entered from the next car, carrying a cup of hot tea.

Since Bishop's compartment was directly adjacent to the connecting doors, the porter walked right into the crisis situation and became a sudden participant.

"What the hell is going—"

He never got the chance to say "on" as the big guy turned the gun from Olivia to the porter, squeezing off a round in his face.

Striking bone, the 9 mm Glaser slug exploded and tore off most of the porter's face, leaving behind a blood-spurting obscenity. The porter sprawled backward against the doors, spilling the contents of the teacup all over himself to wind up thrashing above the tracks between the two cars.

The wiry shooter had turned reflexively but was swinging back around to retarget his original quarry.

Bishop tracked the Ingram on the wiry man and triggered. Blood splattered all over his chest. As

Olivia retreated into the compartment, the big blond guy extended his pistol toward Bishop, pumping the trigger.

Bishop fired again as the wiry shooter hit the deck of the railroad car and he heard the crack of the 9 mm pistol round. It whizzed by his head to shatter the window beside him. A pulse beat later he saw the big guy's face disintegrate much as the porter's had done.

Time suddenly synched back into a normal flow, and Bishop was racing across the car, jumping over the wiry man's body to reach the point where the big blond guy lay thrashing and trying to scream with a mouth that was no longer there.

Inside the compartment Olivia appeared calm. And calm she was, for now, anyway. The screaming would come later; it usually did. Bishop ran toward her and put his arms around her as the compartment filled with passengers. The train ground to a halt, and the shivering that preceded the screams suddenly began.

10

Despite the gusting wind that sent the cold salt spray scudding onto the ferry's deck, most of the crowd on board packed the railings, a universal response of ferry passengers that seemed to defy cultural norms and common sense alike.

As casually attired as the rest of the crowd, jackets covering holstered hardware, Deal Slater and Mason Hawke left the rental to stretch their legs.

Bracing was the word most often used to describe the effects of salt air and wave-tossed mist.

The same applied now as the two covert-warfare specialists leaned against the Mercedes, Slater in tinted aviators and Hawke wearing a ball cap that read Milwaukee Brewers on its front.

Pulling a pack of chewing gum from his jacket pocket, Slater jammed a stick into his mouth as he watched the Ostend wharfs grow small in the distance and the intervening portion of the North Sea become comparatively larger as the ferryboat reached the midway point of its trip.

Like Slater, Hawke was taking in the scenery and the fresh salt air, as well as scanning the crowd out of an operational field "whore's" long-time habit.

His roving glance turned up men in a BMW parked near the end of the line of passenger vehicles near the stern of the ferryboat. For an instant Hawke got the distinct impression that he and Slater were being scoped out and decided in turn to scope out the vehicle and its occupants before disembarking. The body language rarely lied, signifying the presence of watchers as surely as a smoking gun.

Had Hawke been able to eavesdrop on the conversation of the men in the BMW, he would not have remained even mildly complacent. Members of the Hezbollah shooter team code-named Ishtar, the three terrorists had followed the Mercedes through Brussels and onto the ferry.

If possible, they would take down the two U.S. commandos while still on the ferry.

But because their assignment was not for media consumption as the hijacking of an airliner might be, the strike would optimally be carried out in a low-observable fashion according to the two primary rules of engagement for such an action.

The first of these rules called for isolating the target or targets. The second required that the strike force control the killing ground.

The Hezbollah shooters were patient men. They could afford to wait a little longer for those two primary conditions to be satisfied. Then they would strike their quarry and leave dead men behind.

"THE HAIRS ON THE BACK of your neck getting a little prickly?" Slater asked, casually lighting a Sobranie filter cigarette and sticking his arm out the window of the rented Mercedes Hawke drove.

Hawke nodded.

"I was about to ask you the same thing," replied Hawke.

They were now roughly ten kilometers from the ferry landing slip, heading up a stretch of four-lane superhighway that would eventually take them into the Kentish countryside of England and north to London.

Hawke redlined the Mercedes along the excellent four-lane expressway that tied into the M-1 megahighway system stretching from Liverpool to Folkestone.

"See that black Countach, couple car lengths back?" Slater asked.

"You mean the one's been following us for the last thirty or so klicks, right?"

"That's the one, Hawke."

Without saying another word, Hawke switched lanes, almost sideswiping a huge trailer truck loaded with Volvos. The truck driver leaned on his horn and flipped them the bird from six different angles.

The ultrasleek Countach, equipped with aerodynamic spoilers on its rear, was caught short for a split second, but snapped right into lane behind them.

The sports car sped up and almost pulled abreast of the Mercedes. Slater cocked the slide of his Beretta 93-R and prepared to open fire on the driver.

Instead of a weapon-pointing hardman, a kid with long hair flipped them the finger and shot ahead at better than one hundred klicks per hour. "Shit," said Slater. "Almost blew that little wiseass's head off."

"Nerves," Hawke said.

"I copy that," Slater returned.

They were now on the M-1 superhighway heading northeast into London. Slater nodded and was about to speak when Hawke waved him to silence. He had noticed a familiar-looking BMW closing the distance between them at high speed.

The long black snout of a sound suppressor appeared in the window as the driver leaned the barrel of an Italian-made Spectre M96R machine pistol over his left elbow and triggered a burst.

Hawke swerved as a zigzag of steel-jacketed parabellum autofire stitched the Mercedes across its rear left flank.

A wild round ripped into the gas tank of a Toyota sedan to the Mercedes's right.

It went up in a fireball that caused a multiple pileup on the expressway as Hawke highballed the Mercedes out of the crash zone. He took the first turnoff that came up.

Slater hung out the window, firing at the pursuing BMW, but only chewing up the blacktop in front of it.

"Hold on, Slater," Hawke shouted. "We're gonna lose those suckers."

Up ahead was a railroad trestle bridge that paralleled the highway. The bridge forded a steep gorge. The trestle was already partially open.

Hawke double-clutched the Mercedes and shot it over the bridge. The rear tires left the road surface, and the car arced through space. For a heartbeat it looked as if they were not going to make it.

But then, a split second before they would have collided head-on with the concrete bulkhead on the opposite bank, the Mercedes's front wheels grabbed asphalt again, its tires gaining purchase and catapulting the car forward.

The chase vehicle wasn't as lucky or its driver as good.

The BMW almost made the opposite side of the railroad bridge, but unlike the lead vehicle, it crashed head-on into the outer edge of the almost vertical trestle.

Bouncing back, it did a double flip, then slid on its roof down the steep slope of the gorge below, throwing off sparks. There was a loud *crump!* as the fuel lines ruptured and almost immediately caught fire.

In the rearview mirror Hawke could see an orange-black fireball seethe skyward on a pedestal of flame.

Blood slicked the seat to Hawke's side. He realized it was coming from a bad cut on the side of his head where the windshield had imploded.

But it was nothing compared to what the opposition had sustained, and to Mason Hawke, that was enough to make his day.

11

The search, locate and annihilate mission team known as SLAM was one of the covert paramilitary groups established after the gulf war. The mission of these groups was to provide the United States with a credible force in the shadow battlefield of covert warfare that would continue for the remainder of the twentieth century and well beyond.

Unlike other forms of armed conflict, this intense and violent subwarfare would be largely unseen and unreported as a world-shaping global event. But it would be the unseen hand that would drive the engines of politics for decades to come, and in the estimation of the chief executive and his advisers, America could not afford to be without this capability.

A covert presidential finding established the elite and ultrasecret three-man SLAM strike force. It was based on similar tactical formations first deployed by MACV/SOG in Vietnam and Project Phoenix. But it was also based on the fusion cells of Desert

Storm, which swept silently and lethally behind the Iraqi lines to spread terror and destruction.

The SLAM team was underpinned by a large and sophisticated logistics and Intelligence support activity. This network of supercomputers, orbital surveillance platforms, clandestine listening posts and the men and women who monitor them were collectively known as Yellow Light.

The support activity was under the general direction of Admiral Gus Harrington, secretary of defense, who in turn reported directly to the President of the United States and enjoyed the full support of the Joint Special Operations Command.

The sole link between SLAM and the White House—the ligament that fused the sinew of black operations to the bones of administration policy—was former Marine Colonel Jack Callixto, a man who had crawled through the mud and the blood of battlefields from the free-fire zones of Nam to the sand-lashed wasteland of the Arabian desert. Slater, Hawke and Bishop knew they could rely on Callixto under any circumstances, no matter what the politicians and the bean counters might think or say or do.

It was Colonel Callixto who, less than forty-eight hours after the SLAM team had safely returned from the Brussels strike, left his office in the capital and met at a Foggy Bottom parking garage with

Admiral Harrington to discuss the recent turn of events.

"Jack, we got some problems," Harrington told him.

Callixto knew exactly what problems the "old man" was referring to.

Four of the seven shooters killed in thwarted attacks on the SLAM strike crew had been previously spotted at terrorist training camps both in Iran and outside Benghazi, Libya. In three cases the shooters had been conclusively tied to operations launched by the Iranian terrorist organization, Hezbollah.

"You mean the Party of God shooters, right?" Callixto asked.

"Right," the admiral affirmed with a nod. "That's the wild card none of us had expected—that the mullahs in Iran, and probably Khaddafi, too, would move this aggressively to protect the new drug pipeline outside their own backyards."

The admiral handed Callixto a videotape.

"It's all in there, Jack—the reason it's been happening. There's a feverish push under way by the Iranian ruling party to build a facility out in the desert capable of processing weapons-grade fuel. We're still gathering Intelligence data on its significance."

"You suspect it's linked to the narcotrafficking activity we've been seeing?" Callixto asked.

"Yes, frankly, my people do," the admiral affirmed. "And there's something more. You probably have been thinking along the same lines already. Something that ties it all together."

"Right, the mastermind," Callixto replied. "Who exactly is the conduit between the Iranians and the Libyans and probably the Iraqis, too? Who put together all the combinations? I've been running down the list and I come up with only a single name that fits the bill. My only problem is the guy I'm thinking of is supposed to be dead."

"Well, he isn't," the admiral replied. "He's still kicking, Jack. And he's dangerous. Dangerous as all hell."

THE MAN about whom Admiral Harrington and Jack Callixto were conversing was at that moment cleaning his weapon of choice. A Czech Skorpion VZ/63 pistol, it was the one he had used when he had first burst on the scene almost two decades before. He'd emerged as a superstar on the terrorist scene by leading a strike by the Black September Organization at Orly Airport.

Born the son of a well-off Venezuelan physician, he was a man both dedicated to the practice of medicine and an ardent Communist not beloved of the authorities. Despite a doting mother and a household in which he lacked for nothing, the son became consumed with an undying hatred for all authority.

In the sixties the young Venezuelan had traveled to Castro's Cuba, where he was recruited by the Dirección General de Inteligencia, or DGI, and where he impressed the Soviet KGB's talent scouts. Not long afterward he was studying Marxist-Leninist philosophy at Patrice Lumumba Friendship University in Moscow. On graduation he was shuttled to the terrorist training center of George Habash's Black September Organization to serve the cause of Palestinian independence, though not a Palestinian himself.

By the beginning of the 1980s, however, following events that had stunned the world, the terrorist superstar had faded completely from sight. Some claimed that he had been given sanctuary by Moammar Khaddafi, still others that he had been killed by his own treacherous kind. Some asserted that he had altered his appearance and had simply dropped out of sight to let others carry on the battle while retiring to a life of ease.

In reality the story of the man who now inhabited the villa in Tehran had been a mixture of most of these conjectures. He had indeed been given sanctuary, first by the East Germans, then by Khaddafi, and most recently through his friend Abu Nidal, by Saddam Hussein in Iraq. During the gulf war it had been the Iranians who had taken him in. But as he had done before, the terrorist superstar served a variety of masters.

The world had changed a great deal since he had first emerged on the global scene as Carlos—a name not his by birth, but given to him by others. So much so that he sensed the possibility of combining his thirst for violence with his equal thirst for money.

But there was another thirst that the man in the villa possessed, one that had become apparent to a stunned world when they had watched video footage of the terrorist superstar's handiwork during a hijacking episode that culminated in the bloodbath at Entebbe. It was footage that had given the former young revolutionary from Venezuela, who at birth was christened Illich Ramirez Sanchez, another name to go with his best-known alias. From that moment on he had become Carlos the Jackal. And it was now time for the Jackal to slake his sanguine thirst once again.

12

The De Havilland amphibious plane had been supplied by a CIA proprietary outfit based in Majorca, a company that assisted Company field assets besides conducting its normal business activities as a charter company.

The plane had a cruising range of approximately eleven hundred kilometers. It was capable of setting down either on land or on water, its underwing-mounted pontoons affording it the capability of staying afloat even in rough seas.

Sailing under Greek charter, but actually owned by the Libyans behind a variety of dummy corporations, the *Demosthenes IV* was due to enter the port of New York within three days of SLAM's departure from the airfield. The time frame was narrowed for the three-man team by the inherent difficulties in tracking the vessel and launching the search-and-destroy mission once it left the Mediterranean to negotiate the Atlantic Ocean.

Due to a variety of logistical concerns, it was deemed that SLAM's usual method of insertion via military helicopter was nonproductive to the outcome of the mission. Deniability by high government echelons was the chief reason. The strike could never be directly attributed to the intervention of U.S. covert forces.

Hitting the vessel while it was still technically beyond the U.S. sphere of protection—in waters recognized as open to international maritime traffic—was the best path to follow. Pursuing such a course would provide the authorities with a convenient rear-end-saving option. They could blame the ship's destruction on foreign terrorists, drug runners, acts of God, anything they pleased.

Heat that would otherwise come down on the CIA-Pentagon network would be transferred to "the usual suspects."

But mounting an op on the ship within the time frame allocated posed staggering logistical problems. Locating the freighter would be the first and perhaps the most significant problem.

Keyhole-series photoreconnaissance satellites and Big Bird infrared orbital Intelligence platforms had been jockeyed into position to scan the area of ocean through their surveillance "footprints." But a prevailing storm system had put a stalled front with heavy cloud cover over the operational area.

Although the freighter would surely be taking one of several well-mapped and well-traveled commercial routes, it might require days for Slater and his crew to establish the ship's position in many hundreds of kilometers of open ocean.

If SLAM could not locate the *Demosthenes IV* quickly enough, mission and escape time would be cut down to practically zero. There would be no possibility of striking and sending the freighter and its cargo of lethal narcotics permanently to the bottom so as to deflect attention from the powers that had sanctioned the op.

If Slater and his crew could not destroy the heroin freighter, it was almost a foregone conclusion that the ship would be successfully off-loaded and its record-size cargo of Turkish heroin quickly disseminated along the invisible highway of death that had turnoffs into the veins of millions of needle freaks from coast to coast.

Stepped on to decrease its purity and increase its value, the heroin shipment would create thousands of nickel bags and easily realize a combined street value of almost a billion dollars.

It would also rack up a record death toll in lives destroyed by the drug that had traveled thousands of miles from the mountain poppy fields of the Golden Crescent to find a new crop of heroin addicts and ultimately turn them into corpses.

The income produced by the heroin would pour into the numbered bank accounts of the countless parasites who infested the underbelly of society.

From the Mafia to the Chinese triads to the inner-city drug posses who fought their never-ending wars in the streets of America's cities, giving little thought to whom they gunned down in the process, the heroin on board the *Demosthenes IV* would reap a grim toll in human suffering.

But the three men on board the De Havilland were not concerned about the negatives. They would not stop now. Each member of the SLAM team had already made a personal commitment to take the war all the way to its inevitable conclusion.

The destruction of the heroin ship represented different things to each striker on board the amphibious aircraft, but all shared the common goal of taking it down.

EDDIE BISHOP HAD BEEN sweeping the De Havilland in wide, looping arcs across the empty, gunmetal-colored ocean.

Dusk was now falling, and the bronze gong of the sun cast long rays across the ocean as the cloud cover briefly lifted. The sparkling seas of late afternoon would soon be shrouded in darkness as the sun slid behind the horizon.

So far, the SLAM commandos had been unable to eyeball the freighter from their aerial vantage point. They had spotted several merchant vessels that matched the *Demosthenes IV*'s general description and numerous fishing craft, as it was now fishing season in these waters, but none was the ship they searched for.

Then, just before dusk, as they were about to turn back, Slater spotted her steaming due west, her bows glowing a fiery red in the light of the dying sun.

The freighter flew the Greek flag. The vessel's designation was clearly visible through the high-power Bushnell binoculars with which Slater scanned the wrinkling gray sea.

"Take her down," Slater told Bishop, who was at the aircraft's controls. The assault would soon commence.

13

Armed with Colt Commando SMGs, the two contract operatives walked their perimeters on board the rolling deck of the *Demosthenes IV.*

The night was windy, the winds having finally displaced the stalled low-pressure front that had hung over the area. A new cover of scudding lenticular clouds had blown in from the west only an hour before, obscuring the three-quarter moon that would have otherwise brightly lit the sky and the sea.

Although they had officially signed on as merchant seamen, the pair of sailors who patrolled the freighter's deck were in fact mercenaries. Most of the twenty-three-man crew were also either full-time smugglers or free-lance mercs.

Three passengers had booked passage on the freighter when it had put in for an unplanned resupply stop at Valetta, Malta, the previous day.

To take on fuel and medicine was the official explanation for the unscheduled stop in Malta. That would appear in the freighter's log and in the data banks of maritime officials. Actually the three men were the sole reason the ship had made a detour of more than two hundred kilometers from its charted course.

The new passengers were also free-lance operatives. But with a significant difference from their fellow shipmates. The men who had embarked from Malta were not throwaways like the terrorist black assets posing as seamen. Rather the new passengers were experts in what the Intelligence community called "wet jobs," and what the rest of humanity called murder.

The men had been rushed to Malta from New York, London and Cairo when the Libyans had received Intelligence that three highly skilled commandos had disappeared after inflicting enormous damage on the new French Connection drug pipeline's clandestine facilities in both southern France and Brussels.

Still reeling from the staggering blow to their power base in the heart of Europe from the three-man assault team, the honchos of the drug cartel pushed the panic button. The new French Connection's infrastructure had to be salvaged.

Revenues from the Istanbul-Marseilles pipeline had made it possible to dream of an Iranian-Libyan-Iraqi axis that could realize the dream of Pan Arabism through the holy instrument of the Islamic nuclear bomb.

Billions of dollars' worth of drug-generated revenue could be diverted into badly needed weapons projects to fill the power vacuum left by the destruction of Saddam Hussein's once-formidable military machine.

Operation Omar was the key to the Iranian dream of becoming the ruler in a new regional order shaping up in the gulf war's wake, an empire that would encompass Afghanistan and the former Soviet Muslim republics.

To the Iranians and most other governments that needed cash for clandestine ventures, dope was king. It was said that dope had been channeled to the Mafia and the Chinese triads through CIA-controlled conduits in return for the help of those criminal organizations in black-bag jobs that the CIA could never publicly be seen to have a hand in.

Dope was also transported along clandestine highways to the vast neo-Nazi network cobbled together from the survivors of Hitler's Third Reich, which was still the hidden power behind some Third World countries, especially in South and Latin America.

Dope was what had given the Company the power to control those clandestine networks and to bend their corrupt energies toward the will of America. That simply was how things worked in the dirty game of Intelligence, in the real world.

The dirty real world.

And so, by this logic, Operation Omar could use profits derived from narcotrafficking to achieve the imperial ends of Iran: nothing less than the restoration of a once-sprawling Persian empire, much as Saddam Hussein had tried to achieve with the usurpation of Kuwait.

The only thing obstructing these grand designs was the three-man American team that had swept through the operation like raging lions. They had committed so much damage that only the successful conclusion of Omar could offer the hope of damage control and rebuilding. But not even that was a certainty.

To salvage what was left of Omar, the three wet-operations specialists—former triggermen for the East German Stasi—had been mobilized.

Malta had been selected as a rally point, partly because it was the nearest major port to the freighter's current heading. It was also due to the fact that internal-security arrangements with the Maltese government allowed sophisticated weapons and small arms to be brought in—and taken out—whenever necessary, bypassing customs entirely, a primary reason why Malta had long been a staging area for international terrorists.

At Malta, with the right bribes, the watch lists of known operatives that circulated through the customs department branches stationed at major international airports could be ignored. Maltese officials were reputably among the most bribable in the world.

Now the lethal specialists who had come aboard at the Valetta waterfront, unobserved and undetected, waited below the deck of the *Demosthenes IV.* Soon the moment would arrive when their unconventional killing skills would be called upon, and they would erupt into sudden, violent action.

14

The silenced motor on the Zodiac had brought Slater, Bishop and Hawke to within a few hundred meters of the freighter's hull. The ship was moving along at a rough speed of twelve knots in a choppy sea.

Using night observation and magnification devices, the three-man assault team on the Zodiac observed the freighter's deck patrols closely.

Slater estimated that from their position the SLAM strike crew could tie up at or near the aft end of the ship before the patrols' perimeter walk brought them abreast of their position.

Securing the Zodiac to the starboard hull of the big merchant vessel, Slater took the point in the assault on the heroin express.

Silently climbing the iron rungs that projected in a vertical line down the steel hull, Slater crouched beyond the gunwale and began his recon of the strike zone.

The foredeck of the freighter was deserted, the flat profile to port and starboard broken only by the dark silhouettes of masts and tarp-covered containerized cargo.

Signaling to Bishop and Hawke to hang back on the Zodiac, Slater sprinted across the deck and took cover behind a large steel funnel. In a few moments one of the perimeter walkers passed his position.

Slater moved quickly.

The combat-tested Ka-bar knife was already in his fist, the razor tip jabbed into the soft spot beneath the right ear and twisted savagely to destroy the motion and breathing centers of the brain. The guard went rag doll limp, and Slater dragged the corpse behind a row of palleted containers.

Slater signaled to the others with his index finger that he had taken out the sentry.

Bishop and Hawke nodded and silently ascended to the deck, becoming shadows that merged with the deeper shadows cast by the architecture of the fore-deck.

From a watertight pouch, Slater produced a long assault weapon finished in nonreflective black. Working quickly, he affixed a stubby cylinder finished in the same matte black onto the weapon's muzzle. The weapon was an FN Minimi 5.56 mm machine gun, its military designation the M249 squad auto weapon, or SAW. Slater had selected the Minimi for several reasons. At an unloaded weight of only fourteen pounds, five ounces, and measur-

ing a compact thirty inches with its buttstock in col-
lapsed position, the Minimi had both weight and
size working in its favor.

The Minimi was capable of unleashing steel tum-
blers from its barrel at a variable cycling rate of 750
to 1250 rounds per minute. The lightness of the
weapon contributed to its lethality. So light it could
be fired one-handed, the Minimi was as controllable as a conventional assault weapon even in full-
auto mode.

For the night operation assault role for which
Slater had selected the Minimi, the bell-shaped flash
suppressor, normally fitted at the end of its barrel,
had been removed so that the Hush Puppy-type si-
lencer could be added. Two turns of a ridged metal
thumbscrew, and the Hush Puppy was securely affixed to the Minimi's barrel.

In the few seconds it had taken Slater to deploy
his lethal full-auto armament, Bishop and Hawke
had fanned out to take on their prearranged tasks in
priming the freighter for destruction.

The charges of C-4 plastic explosive were slotted
at key points around the deck perimeter. Then electrical detonator fuzes were inserted into each charge
and the compact electronic timers calibrated.

The charges were set to detonate only a few minutes after the trio was scheduled to escape the
doomed ship via the Zodiac. The margin for error

was slim, but the SLAM specialists were taking no chances.

The ship had to be blown to smithereens, even if SLAM's tight operational time frame increased the probability that the commando unit would be sent to the bottom right along with her.

Deployment of the plastic charges was slated for six minutes. Hawke and Bishop completed this phase of the assault operation in just under four, and thirty seconds later linked up with Slater.

Ten seconds later the second perimeter walker's patrol brought him abreast of the assault crew just as all three reached the rally point.

The patrol's eyes widened in panic as he saw the combat-garbed shapes bulking large from the shadows.

After the initial shock, he raised the Commando SMG and fired at the intruders. He was too slow, however. A low-decibel, automatic burst from the Minimi sent the terminated contract operative crumpling to the deck.

The body count now stood at two and rising.

At a nod from Slater, Bishop and Hawke tossed the cold-smoked merc overboard, dumping his discarded weapon into the drink with him.

Slater peeled back the black Velcro Tekna strip that concealed the crystal of his Tag-Huer chronometer, preventing the possibility of give-away glare.

Mission time was already ten minutes old.

It had another ten to go.

SLAM's commanding officer signaled toward the hatchway nearby that led below decks.

Slater's teammates proceeded to initiate phase two of their preemptive strike.

15

The freighter's hold was illuminated dimly by overhead incandescent floodlights.

From the amount of hull that had been visible above the waterline on the strike team's initial recon of the freighter, it was evident that her hold was not filled to capacity.

This proved to be the case on closer inspection. The hold, in fact, carried very little in the way of cargo. Most of what it did carry was packed in crates, not containers. It did not take long to locate the crates containing the heroin.

The crates contained Sicilian reliquaries known as *incantesimos*. The *incantesimos* were common trappings of religious services in southern Italy and Malta. The point of origin on the crates was listed as Palermo, Sicily.

Cracking open one of the *incantesimos*, Slater found what could well be termed pay dirt.

A one-kilo oblong plastic bag of Turkish brown heroin was packed tightly within the hollow interior of each of the ancient Sicilian religious objects.

A quick head count revealed that there were approximately a dozen Sicilian reliquaries within each of the dozen crates. It didn't take an Einstein to figure the total weight of the heroin shipment at one hundred forty-four kilos.

An incredible amount of pure, unadulterated skag, even for the brown Turkish variety, which was by no means as pure as the best triple-nine China White or even the new Colombian White that had been hitting the streets in recent months.

Still, by all estimates, one heck of a haul.

Stepped on four times, as was the normal practice in adulterating pure heroin to street quality, each bag would be potentially worth five figures in drug revenues.

If the quality was high enough, each kilo bag might be stepped on five, six or even eight times, significantly increasing its monetary yield on the street.

While Slater again pulled sentry duty, Bishop and Hawke slotted the ship's hold with C-4 charges, also set to blow after a narrow delay factor.

After five minutes, the hold of the contraband freighter was completely primed for destruction. Throughout the ship, SLAM had slotted shaped plastic demo charges designed to multiply the concussive force of the plastic explosive many times over.

Any single charge would be sufficient to rip a gaping hole in the plate-steel hull of the freighter. Combined, the explosive force of the charges would be sufficient to blow the ship right out of the water, so that only pieces of the ship would be left to sink bottomward.

It was deliberate overkill on SLAM's part. The less evidence that remained of the *Demosthenes IV* and her cargo, the better.

"Let's get out of here," Slater whispered to his two companions.

Unfortunately this quickly turned out to be easier said than done.

Sudden death was arriving on the scene.

THE EX-STASI TRIGGERMEN on board the freighter were waiting for the assault team amidships.

They had staged a predawn patrol of their own after a crewman, while relieving himself on deck, had stumbled on the fallen crewman.

Awakened in their cabins, the specialists were mission capable in moments. They had been expecting this contingency for a long time.

One on one, three on three.

The clock was ticking. Ground zero was imminent, and the kills had nowhere left to go but hell.

The first merc terminator moved fast yet with an economy of motion that only an individual born with special athletic gifts and who engaged in constant training could ever bring to bear. Tucking sideways, he fired his Commando SMG in a controlled burst at Hawke.

Lethal pulses of autofire spanged off the metal deck plate, almost taking him out.

Hawke was fast, though. And lucky to boot.

Scrambling for cover, the SLAM commando cut loose with an answering burst of the Sionic-silenced MP/5-10 he ported, pockmarking the plate steel and sending the merc for cover.

Bishop, meanwhile, chased the third merc terminator—who was armed with a Jati SMG—across the main deck to the raised aft deck near the stern.

The mercenary dived for cover, tucked to a crouch and raised the Jati, cutting loose with a burst of 9 mm white heat that blew the Heckler & Koch SMG from Bishop's hand and damned near took the hand away with it.

As the merc raised the autoweapon to trigger a burst across Bishop's belly, Bishop lashed out with a toe kick that evened the score, sending the lightweight plastic-framed Jati skittering across the deck, to be swallowed by the darkness.

The merc sprang to his feet with catlike quickness. A knife appeared in his hand. He swung the blade back and forth. Bishop recognized the blade and frowned.

Only the truly bad used the kind of blade the merc had pulled on him. To anybody but a pro blades- man, that particular cutlery was more liability than asset.

The knife was long and thin. A Fairbairn-Sykes dagger, designed for only one purpose: to kill. In the hands of an expert, the dagger was the deadliest hand weapon there was, second only to a gun. Bishop had to move carefully and quickly or his life would be over.

Feinting left, the merc terminator whipped the dagger in a darkly glittering arc that would have sliced Bishop from hip to nipple had he not stepped back to avoid the vicious swipe.

Pivoting to deliver a comeback kick, Bishop was unable to take advantage of the awkward stance that usually followed a power-lunge with a knife.

The bladesman was good enough to have made the lunge with an economy of body motion, keep- ing his center of gravity low and using only his arms and shoulders to deliver the strike.

He had recovered his balance almost immedi- ately.

The bladesman smiled and quickly took the of- fensive again. His hand was lost in a flashing blur of speed as he launched another death strike. The slash was high, aimed at the base of Bishop's throat.

Bishop had been waiting for the next offensive, and had been ready to deal with the strike when it came. He knew that up against a veteran blade swinger, only speed and an effective counterattack stood any chance of success.

Sidestepping the thrust to his neck, he countered with a slashing knuckle-punch combo that landed solidly on the bladesman's face and upper body, rocking him backward, stunned and badly hurt.

Dazed though he was, the man made a quick recovery. But he was shaken and injured. His movements had now lost the crispness, speed and spare economy that had kept him on the offensive and unhurt so far.

Another power kick by Bishop landed with crushing impact on the merc's forearm, snapping the long, thin bones across which muscle tissue was tightly strung.

The merc cried out from the excruciating pain and transferred the knife to his good hand for a last-ditch lunge at his opponent.

Hurling himself at Bishop, he used all his remaining physical reserves to rush his smaller but more powerfully built opponent and try to stab him.

Still strong and fast despite his injuries, he almost made it.

The SLAM commando deflected the strike, but the merc's fury sent both men tumbling to the deck in a flailing tangle of arms and legs.

From that moment on it became a contest of strength, endurance and skill as both men grappled on the freighter's aft upper deck.

The grim contest ended with brutal suddenness only when Bishop managed to wrestle the blade away from the merc and thrust it with vicious finality into his throat.

The corpse was heavy as Bishop rolled it away and sprang to his feet. Then the sound of a firefight on the foredeck made Bishop turn around.

16

Amidships, on the main deck below Bishop, Slater and Hawke were pinned by gunfire from two henchmen hunkering behind stacks of containers lashed down aft of the freighter's bows.

Their positions gave the mercs a tactical edge, even if Slater's Minimi still denied the aggressors the critical advantage of superior firepower.

But if Slater and Hawke moved from cover, the shooters could nail them. Unfortunately the converse was not true.

Slater and Hawke were trading fire with men who were well covered and could afford to wait, even fall back to safer positions without becoming easy targets.

Grasping the situation from his position aft, Bishop grabbed his fallen opponent's Jati SMG to replace his damaged H&K and sighted on one of the mercs whose back was partially exposed behind a mast.

Bishop realized that the range wasn't good.

The ex-Stasi's Commando SMGs would give them the advantage in a firefight. Bishop had to close the gap between them in order to use the 9 mm Jati effectively.

And close it fast.

Moving stealthily down the metal stairs to the main deck, Bishop tried to get within range of the Jati's parabellum ammo. But there were too many obstacles between him and his targets.

The layout of the deck would require him to sprint across too many stretches of open space. If he did so he'd have poor cover and might be nailed by the opposition without even having an opportunity to return fire. He didn't stand a chance that way.

Then Bishop looked up at the block and tackle that stretched from the winch overhead to the tall steel mast atop which the ship's barometer and other weather gear was located. He continued up the metal stairs onto the aft deck.

Grabbing hold of the block and tackle and kicking out, he launched himself over the edge of the railing and out into space.

Bishop let go precisely at the farthest point of the swing and made a two-point landing behind the contract shooter who'd presented himself as a target a few minutes before.

Reflexively bringing up his Commando SMG, the terminator whirled to face the sudden presence behind him.

Bishop kicked out, delivering a lashing blow to the face of the merc.

The blow was so powerful and struck at such an angle that it snapped his head back on his neck, severely fracturing the upper spinal cord and causing him to drop his weapon as he sagged to the deck.

Only one kill specialist was still left.

The gunman, behind some containerized cargo, was firing his automatic weapon at Slater. The SLAM commando dodged by tucking left and compacting his body into a hard-to-hit ball. A storm of 9 mm bullets chased him as he rolled out of the sweeping line of fire and ducked behind a large cast-iron deck funnel.

The contract shooter had fumbled. By targeting Slater, he had exposed himself.

It wasn't an easy shot, but the Minimi had the range and the firepower to catch the merc full on the chest and stitch him across the torso from clavicle to hip, causing almost instantaneous death.

"Hustle!" Slater shouted as the final target dropped.

Bishop and Hawke didn't need to be told twice. They sprinted for the gunwales of the ship, dodging ineptly aimed fire launched from the surviving crewmen on the bridge. These throwaway mercs were evidently used to firing at sharks, not human targets.

Bishop and Hawke hustled over the side of the vessel and into the Zodiac while Slater laid down suppressing fire that forced the shooters on the bridge to seek cover.

Hawke was starting up the Zodiac's silenced engine even as Slater was jumping into the inflatable rubber boat.

The black vulcanized attack craft sprinted away from the enormous ship as fire from the bullpups and hand cannons packed by the crew on board peppered the water with lead.

The Zodiac was only a few hundred meters from the freighter when it blew sky-high.

The concussion was earsplitting.

The primary explosions sent a fireball ballooning up into the black night sky and casting hellish reflections on the gunmetal waters of the darkened Mediterranean.

A few beats later the plastic explosive demolition charges that the strike team had planted below decks detonated with waves of pulsed concussions that were fiercer still.

The freighter broke apart, then disintegrated. Its thousands of cubic tons of steel hull dissolved in the incandescent mushroom cloud that reared up on a great shaft of fire and smoke like some angry sea god.

As the Zodiac sped away from ground zero, the rumbling began to fade like distant thunder.

Floating chunks of burning debris littered the surface of the sea for kilometers in all directions, belching up smoke into the eerily moonlit darkness just before dawn.

Deal Slater looked at the two men beside him as they approached the De Havilland aircraft, which lay anchored, afloat on pontoon wings.

No one spoke. The action had left them drained.

For now extraction from the strike zone was priority one.

PART TWO:

Special Recon

17

Through the worsening storm, the MH-53J Pave Low helicopter flew under the curtain, its forward-looking infrared terrain-mapping system—FLIR—allowing it to hug the nap of the earth in a manner few other aircraft its size were capable of imitating.

At a little past 0500 hours zulu it had lifted from the aft deck of the Navy frigate *Southampton,* which was standing to off the coast of Malta.

On board the Pave Low were Slater and his men, who were following the heroin pipeline to its source.

At Izmir, Turkey, and at Buca—the team's secondary target zone—important way stations were located. These sites needed to be dismantled, like the other targets SLAM had struck on its whirlwind round of interdiction missions.

Rain was falling in canting sheets as the chopper rose above the wrinkled hills of the Taurus Range along the Turkish coast.

FLIR saw through the storm cell, and the two big five-hundred-horsepower General Electric engines that powered the Pave Low were not affected in the least by the gusting winds approaching speeds of twenty knots.

Indeed, the storm provided additional cover as the chopper made its run low along the coastal plain and over the mountainous range rising up just behind it.

Soon the Pave Low's drop manager received a confirm on the LZ. She notified the three covert strikers that the Pave Low was getting into position for the drop.

"Go!" she said, flashing the team leader a thumbs-up.

Slater was first, speed rappeling down the guy line that extended from the rear of the chopper. Hawke came down behind him, his pack somewhat bulkier due to the Satcom satellite communications radio gear he carried. It would be used later to call the Pave Low for extraction.

The last member of the commando penetration force out, Eddie Bishop rappeled down, his H&K MP/5-10 SMG tracking left and right through the rain as he slid to earth.

Already in position, the door gunners stood behind the General Electric Miniguns, tracking the 7.62 mm weapons to cover the team.

Slater, Hawke and Bishop could still feel the rotor wash from the chopper's powerful engines as they hustled away from the low-hovering helicopter. Then they watched as the big military craft as-

cended from its low hover as rivulets of cold rain ran down its riveted flanks.

Before long it vanished into the dark sky, and SLAM vanished into the mud and the night and the rain.

WITH THE PASSAGE of the storm, SLAM was several klicks away from the landing zone. The shadow warriors were slowly working across rugged mountain country similar to that of northern Afghanistan.

Their target was a valley in the steep foothills of the Taurus Range where Keyhole satellites had pinpointed the site of a major poppy field and heroin-processing complex.

Adjoining the fields were some old ruins. They were the remains of an old hill town that had been abandoned during the nationalist fighting of the 1920s. Ethnic minorities had clashed prior to the establishment of the Kemal Ataturk government, and large areas of the countryside were depopulated as a result.

Amid the cracked and gutted shells of long-abandoned buildings and the narrow, rubble-strewn streets of the once-thriving hill town named Anouk, the new French Connection had established a drug-processing facility utilizing state-of-the-art equipment. The heroin cartel had colonized the ruins much like a fungus that grows on decaying matter.

Local villagers were employed—as they had been for centuries—in harvesting the poppy crop from which the heroin base was derived.

Proceeding toward its target in the darkness of early morning, the SLAM team moved leapfrog fashion across the flat expanse of a high mountain pass.

On high alert for hostile patrols, Slater and his crew kept their automatic weapons in an unsafed state, set on burst-fire mode.

The three strikers did not proceed in a single column but instead moved spread out across the steeply rising terrain in a triangular patrol formation. Bishop took the point as scout, and Slater and Hawke formed the triangle's base.

Unlike the jungles of the Golden Triangle, where SLAM had previously fought, the terrain here was open and the vegetation sparse.

Because of the nature of the semiarid type of operational environment and thanks to their night-vision goggles, the three SLAM operatives were able to maintain constant visual contact. This was augmented by regular position checks using the AN/PRC-3000 communicators, signaling at preconfigured rally points situated along their line of march.

A little before dawn, the strike team was midway to their destination point, moving with the storm.

ON BOARD THE FRIGATE *Southampton,* the battle-systems officer consulted his main computer screen for a final status check.

The mission clock was ticking. If he did not receive an abort from the skipper, the countdown to deployment of the weapon system would continue unimpeded.

Deployment had to be perfect and it would be.

The coordinates for the weapons system had been downloaded from satellite photoreconnaissance that had been processed at the CIA's national photographic interpretation center.

The finest technical people in the business had made certain that every byte of code was accurate, every pixel of digitized information matched the target profile as snugly as a suit from a Hong Kong tailor.

But the battle-systems officer checked and recalibrated just the same.

It was his show, after all, and he did not want anything to go wrong. Not just for his own sake, but for the sake of the three men on the ground, who could wind up at the center of a fiery whirlwind should even a single calibration be less than perfect.

18

By now the strike team no longer needed night-vision goggles. The meager light of a cold mountain dawn was spreading across the bleak semiarid landscape.

Slater and his crew were negotiating the final approach to their primary reconnaissance area. Their mission time schedule called for remaining there throughout daylight and scouting out any activity in the vicinity in order to finalize their strike plan before commencing the op.

The SLAM team had dug a spider hole in a shallow depression below a rocky rise some time before sunup.

The spider hole was spacious and comfortable enough for the trio to spend the next ten to twelve hours in. Covered by camouflage netting, it was well concealed.

First watch duty fell to Slater, while Bishop grabbed some rest and chow. Hawke would get some rest, as well, but not before he transmitted a position report via satellite to the mission-support facility code-named Playboy.

Hawke planted the Satcom's compact dish antenna in the soft dirt of Izmir by means of its tripod legs.

Hawke had programmed the transmission times to the three-and-a-half-ton Ferret-class SIGINT satellite, a Magnus orbital listening post positioned some thirty thousand kilometers in high, circumpolar orbit.

Even relatively faint electrical energy emissions could be picked up by Magnus's two hundred-meter-long antennae, which trailed from the satellite like the tendrils of some giant space-faring jellyfish.

These emissions, produced by all nonhardened electronic equipment, were known collectively by the code name Tempest and were the subject of the National Security Agency's unwavering scrutiny.

Using Magnus and its electronic cousins, NSA was capable of monitoring cellular phone transmissions across the globe. A sophisticated NSA computer, designed by Seymour Cray, combed and filtered the electronic environment for key words useful to the Intelligence listeners.

But Magnus and its relatives were useful also in the area of covert field communications, and it was to this purpose that the SIGINT platform in high overhead orbit would be put as the countdown proceeded.

When the Satcom had informed Hawke that the device had locked on to the orbiting Magnus spy satellite, Hawke began his transmission using the call sign Hammerhead.

Seconds later the NSA listening post in Ankara, Turkey, acknowledged Hawke's situation report.

The brief encrypted exchange was terminated after Hawke informed the listening post to await another sitrep prior to the team's extraction from the mission zone. Hawke ETA'd this extraction at approximately 0500 hours the following day.

Having concluded his transmission, Hawke broke down the Satcom rig and stowed the two modular components in his rucksack.

Feeling hungry, Hawke broke out an MRE package and selected one featuring what Uncle Sam labeled "creamed chicken, mashed potatoes and apple-crumb pie."

The chow did, Hawke had to admit, taste somewhat less like plastic foam than the MREs of Desert Storm vintage, referred to only half-jokingly by some line grunts as "meals rejected by Ethiopia." However, Army chow still had a long way to go before it was as palatable as a TV dinner.

Forking some of the creamed chicken into his mouth, Hawke reflected that during World War II one of the most prized spoils of war by American dogfaces were German rations, which included wine, cheese and ham.

Some things never changed, Hawke mused as he finished his meal, bagged the refuse for disposal and joined Bishop in getting some much-needed sack time, grateful that the final watch duty had fallen to him.

Used to grabbing shut-eye in tough places, Hawke was soon fast asleep.

THE CHILLED RAIN that had characterized SLAM's mission-zone penetration had begun again by mid-morning, starting as a sprinkle but soon soaking the parched semiarid landscape.

From his position as lookout, Deal Slater massaged his strained eyes and again raised the thirty-power Bushnell field glasses to his face.

Their nonreflective lenses made detection hard, while desert ghillie cover and camo face paint camouflaged Slater's head.

He placed the black rubber eyepieces against the sockets of his eyes as he heard fat drops of rain strike the protective cover of the hole with an increasing tempo.

Protected from the rain by the netting, the Bushnells had revealed to Slater a consistent pattern of activity in and around the ruined hill town.

Heavy trucks churned up the mud-sucking dirt road, off-loading one cargo, loading another, then setting out again. The cargo being trucked up the hill was composed of raw materials for the heroin-processing operation while the processed base was coming down again. This pattern had been firmly established through satellite recon of the area prior to the commando drop.

The poppy fields that supplied the raw materials for the semirefined product lay beside the town, and these were patrolled by AK-toting guards.

There was no harvesting activity yet, and a glance at the crop in the field had told Slater why this was so. The poppies were still in flower, and the egg-sized, greenish tan pods swelling just beneath them were not yet ripe enough to permit harvesting.

In a matter of days, though, the crop would be ripe enough to bring in, and an army of hill people hired as migrant workers would descend on the valley like locusts, first slitting the pods to allow the pungent, milky opium sap to flow, then returning to scrape off the sap.

As the drenching rain let up, giving way to a cloud-filled afternoon sky, Slater compiled a detailed assessment of the numbers of men in the hill town and their state of combat readiness.

He estimated that no more than thirty-five men were on the site, and only a dozen of these were professionals, perhaps gaining their experience in training camps in Benghazi, Libya or across the Turkish border in neighboring Iran.

The majority of these assets, however, were local thugs, hastily recruited and handed small arms. All such foot soldiers would be ranked expendable and their loyalty never trusted, though they performed tasks like guard duty, which the elite cadres did not relish.

Soon Bishop relieved Slater and he joined Hawke for some much-needed rest.

Bishop and then Hawke kept up a constant surveillance on the mountain stronghold for the rest of the day and then into the night. When Slater rotated back to standing lookout, it was already well past midnight.

By now the occupants of the ruined hill town were settling down for the night as the rain returned, bringing with it a damp chill. The activity level decreased in the drug facility thanks, in part, to the weather.

The opposite was the case with the men in the camo BDUs who waited in their lonely outpost on the muddy side of an overlooking hill.

They were rested and ready to consolidate their mission assignment.

19

Faces striped with nonreflective camo, wearing armored vests and fingerless tactical gloves, weapons cocooned in flexible netting material, SLAM mobilized from the spider hole.

Prior to moving from their down position, their encampment had been completely sanitized. All disposables had been bagged and buried and the hole completely covered so that no visible trace remained.

The rain had not abated. As the SLAM team moved through the fields of swaying poppies, rain of moderate intensity fell with a steady cadence, and the rich odors of wet earth mingled with the turpentine smell of the field of meter-high plants.

With little to hold it together, the dry earth had quickly turned into a muddy quagmire. But mud was as universal a constant in field operations as was death, and Slater, Hawke and Bishop didn't complain as they slogged on.

In addition to the MP/5-10 SMGs ported by all three strikers, Bishop and Hawke were equipped with Maremont M-60 light machine guns for additional firepower.

The lightweight M-60E3 Maremont machine guns—much improved carbine versions of the original Vietnam-era M-60—were equipped with 100-round box mags containing NATO standard 7.62 mm hardball ammo.

Every fourth bullet on the feed belt was a tracer round. Apart from permitting SLAM's two squad gunners to accurately tape their targets, the tracers would also create a vortex effect of luminous green when fired.

SLAM had found that the psychological effect of the tracer loads enhanced the terror that their sudden appearance struck into the hearts and minds of the opposition.

With all weapons unsafed, SLAM skirted the poppy field under cover of darkness and rain, their jump boots deep in sucking Turkish mud.

TWO SENTRIES STOOD OUT against the backdrop of the target site.

The SLAM team watched as the two men warmed their hands from the heat of an oil drum filled with burnable trash.

The men were smoking hand-rolled cigarettes containing strong local tobacco mixed with hashish, paying far more attention to their creature comforts than their perimeter-patrol duties.

After months of walking their perimeters, the watchers had grown complacent and careless. The shadows no longer held any terror for them, and when the rain and the chill bit into a man's flesh, warming one's hands over the fire took precedence.

Their AKR machine guns were positioned where they would do the least good.

One sentry had his weapon slung across his back, while another sentry's weapon lay in the mud not far from where he stood, by turns breathing onto his hands and passing them back and forth across the fire.

Using hand signs—a fist clenched twice, followed by pointed index fingers an equal number of times—Slater gestured for Bishop to take out the two sentries. Bishop nodded and handed his Maremont to Slater, who slung it across his back.

The H&K SMGs had the range and the firepower to deal with the hostiles and, unlike the M-60E3s, they also bore Hush Puppy-type sound suppressors.

Slater and Hawke watched as Bishop loped on a crouch along the field toward the base of the ruins where the two opposition personnel were highlighted by the flames from the burning trash.

He had to crawl through the mud on his belly for the last three hundred meters or so in order to get into position behind them. As he stealthily crept up on his targets he decided to use a pop-up maneuver and attack them frontally. He stopped and made a final scan when he was approximately twenty meters from his targets.

He scanned the surrounding structures, too, in case the sentry post was itself the subject of scrutiny by concealed watchers.

Bishop saw no other watchers, though, and he grasped the MP/5-10, its fire-select lever studded to full auto, its safety flipped from the safe position.

Moments later he was popping up from amid the sea of flowers and bringing the SMG into violent play.

As he aimed at the two assets, stunned expressions crossed their faces. The one with the AKR slung across his back contorted to make a desperate grab for the weapon.

A trigger squeeze sent two bursts of 10 mm steel-jackets cycling out of the H&K.

The system of gas-shearing mechanisms inside the stubby cylinder of the Hush Puppy suppressor made the rounds exit with only a series of muffled wheezes.

The one holding the AKR was knocked backward as a trio of slugs ripped open his chest, exposing a carmine mass of flayed viscera.

The other man took the second burst in the side and keeled sideways with hands outflung. The burst had torn his heart to shreds, and he lay on his face with arterial blood pumping out onto the rain-soaked ground.

The entire confrontation from trigger pull to termination took less than two minutes. Bishop gave the area another quick scan and determined that the killing ground was not under an observer's eyes.

Holding the MP/5-10 in one hand, he reached for the AN/PRC-3000's transmit stud with his other and depressed it twice, the two clicks in their ears signaling to Slater and Hawke that they were cleared to advance.

In a matter of minutes, Bishop's SMG was again riding its mount on his pack while the Maremont 7.62 mm weapon was firmly gripped in his tactical-gloved hands.

With Slater on point with his silenced MP/5-10 and Bishop and Hawke bringing up the rear, the strike team mobilized to penetrate and obliterate the Izmir target.

They proceeded with their usual outstanding fieldcraft. Moving singly and pausing at intervals to reconnoiter, the team deployed on the site with practiced stealth.

Slater took the point while covered by Bishop and Hawke, progressing toward the shadowed exterior of the largest of the building ruins, the one their recon had indicated was the main center of activity.

It was near there that the strike team encountered an unexpected setback.

20

The opposition asset popped out of a narrow alley between two gutted buildings. That he'd been relieving himself against a wall was apparent from the actions of his hands at his fly.

Already in the open, Slater had no choice but to freeze as the merc appeared in the small flagstone courtyard that had probably once been the town's main square.

Sometimes they didn't see you.

But this wasn't one of those times.

Despite the AKR that the ground asset carried with its leather strap wound loosely around his wrist, Slater saw that he was just a kid. He stopped short as his glance fell on the shadowy figure standing in the open.

He blinked and did a half take, thinking that he was seeing things. Then, as he realized that his eyes were telling the truth, his stunned mind took stock of the grave danger he was in.

Slater had no choice but to take him down. A silenced burst of 10 mm H&K fire to the belly knocked the merc down to the broken flagstones of the square.

Signaling to Hawke and Bishop to remain in the shadows, Slater ran toward the body and began dragging it into one of the shadowed streets. He felt exposed as he did this and knew he was in a tactically unsound position. Moments later this uneasy sense was confirmed as Slater saw a door open off to one side of the square.

In a spill of light from the interior of the dwelling there stood a figure, larger around the middle and older than the dead youth.

"Hamid!" cried the newcomer. "Where the hell are you?"

In one hand he held a bottle of wine and he paused to raise it to his lips and take a long pull.

"Hamid!" he cried again, and stepped out into the flagstone path where Slater was crouched over the body of the merc he'd just taken down.

The drunken man continued into the square and spotted Slater. Going for the gun at his hip, he dropped the bottle of wine to the flagstones. It shattered with a noise that sounded like thunder in the stillness of the ruins, broken only by the patter of the steady mountain rain.

The older opposition asset had the 7.62 mm pistol half out of its holster before a sound-suppressed burst from Bishop in the shadows cut him down. He died, but not before bellowing like a slaughtered bull as he slumped to the bloodied flagstones.

The sounds in the night produced their predictable results. Moments later the barking of nervous dogs and the shouts of surprised men echoed through the derelict mountain hamlet.

Lights were coming on in the windows of the partially intact stone structures surrounding the square. Like it or not, the strike zone had just turned white-hot, and SLAM would have to ride with the tide of battle.

Slater, Bishop and Hawke reacted quickly as mission-honed combat reflexes took over. Linking up back-to-back in a defensive formation, they raised their automatic weapons and unleashed rotoring 7.62 mm steel against the mercs who spilled out of the ruins in a cursing, shouting mass.

The moving wall of steel mowed down most of the first wave of assailants. Seeing their comrades go down, latecomers to the fray developed a sudden sense of caution and fell into defensive positions to answer the intruders' fire with salvos of their own.

Any standoff could not prove favorable to SLAM, and so Slater ordered an immediate fighting pullout.

"Let's do it now!" Slater yelled, and pointed toward the main refinery building only a few meters away. "Use the satchel charges."

The charges would be set to blow in seconds. While Hawke and Bishop covered him, Slater set the charges for a twenty-second delay period and hurled two of the musette bags filled with high explosive through a window frame of the refinery building nearby.

Flashes of white light strobed through the town square as the charges went off with a deafening bang. Blast overpressure sent tongues of fire licking out over the scorched-black masonry as pulses of energy thundered in the night.

To a distance of thirty meters out from the epicenter of the blast, the earth trembled from the effects of the detonations. But within seconds the booming charges faded, and 7.62 mm small-arms fire began to chatter.

Slater, Hawke and Bishop staged a fighting withdrawal from the center of the blast site, the bolt clatter of their fast-cycling automatic weapons in grim counterpoint to the heavier, slower thudding of the AKs fielded by the opposition assets who were firing from protected positions in the ruins.

By now the refinery was burning steadily as Slater and his crew made for the heavy trucks in the parking area. The team had intended to walk out, but recent developments had made that impossible.

While Hawke worked to get the truck started and Bishop sent rotoring fire licking out, Slater unshipped an AT-4 LAW rocket from the holdalls securing it to his pack.

Hawke got the vehicle started after a few unproductive tries and Slater and Bishop hopped on board. As they rolled from the compound, throwing answering fire at the shooters hunkered in the ruins, Slater pointed the LAW tube at the other center of the facility, the ammo dump, and let fly the round. Back blast whooshed from the rear of the shoulder-mounted launcher tube and dissipated over the sides of the uncovered vehicle.

The warhead exploded with a clap of thunder and a shower of sparks as the high-explosive shell burst against the walls of the ruined structures. Walls of ancient brick caved in, and the munitions inside the dump cooked off. Rockets flew off into the air, corkscrewing against the night as the ground trembled.

Now, as the truck roared down the steep access road, Slater picked up Hawke's idle Maremont and hurled suppression fire at the ground assets who were shooting at them. Moments later the weapons fire from the town had faded into a lull.

But the firing resumed as the ground assets hustled into vehicles and proceeded to give furious chase.

21

Bishop fired steadily from the Maremont as the two-and-a-half-ton truck gained the flat base of the steep slope. As Hawke floored the gas to pick up speed, Slater unshipped another of the team's LAW AT-4s from Bishop's pack and began to deploy the light armor weapon.

Hefting it to his shoulder, he retracted the AT-4's pop-up sight and squinted against the launcher tube's rubber eyepiece. Framed in the cross reticle was one of the two chase vehicles. Centering it in the LAW's sights, Slater squeezed the trigger, and the high-explosive warhead began its lethal course.

As the round left the pipe, Slater could feel it buck on his shoulder, a rush of back blast billowing harmlessly into the night air as the truck juddered over the uneven and muddy mountain terrain.

A pulse beat later the HEAT round struck the first vehicle dead on. It was a direct hit in the center of the grille.

The jet of semimolten steel traveling at roughly twenty-seven thousand feet per second tore open the engine block, and pieces of the wrecked front end went pinwheeling into the air.

For a moment the white-out effect of the burst masked the round's violent effects on the occupants of the vehicle. When the flare faded, it was apparent that one of them had been set afire by spilled fuel from the vehicle's ruptured storage tanks. Cocooned in crackling flames, the human torch raced madly into the darkness before toppling to the ground and thrashing as the devouring fire turned the body into a carbonized mass.

Hefting up the Maremont, Slater joined Bishop in pouring a vortex of green tracers into the second vehicle, which had pulled short of the flaming wreckage. Mounted on its back was a .50-caliber heavy-barreled gun on a pintle stand.

The tail gunner began at once to unleash a sustained burst of large-caliber tracer rounds. He didn't last long. Cut down by a burst of 7.62 mm rounds, he went tumbling rag-doll fashion from the scout vehicle, and the gun fell silent.

A pulse beat later the driver caught a round in the heart. In death spasms he wrenched the steering wheel sideways, sending the vehicle careering off the shoulder of the road, where it jackknifed, flipped and came to rest on its side with its wheels spinning.

Of the pursuers there was only a single survivor. A burst from the Maremont caught him as he broke for the cover of the darkness beyond the road. He went sprawling to the rocky ground, where the rain washed steadily down on his bloodied body.

Instructing Bishop to keep the Maremont pointing from the back of the truck, Slater went to the front of the truck and rapped on the window at the rear of the cab. At the top of his lungs he was able to communicate to Hawke to pull over and stop the vehicle.

"How close are we to transmission time?" Slater asked the team's technical officer.

"Ten minutes," Hawke replied after consulting his wrist chronometer. "I'll begin setting up," he went on. "There's a good spot near that rise up ahead."

Telling Bishop to stand guard with the final LAW AT-4 and the Maremont, Slater got behind the wheel of the truck.

Putting the rig into gear, he swung the heavy transport around to a rock outcropping opposite a road that ran into the hill country. Slater was confident that the truck was well concealed from the road.

He climbed back down from the cab and was soon at Bishop's position. Squatting, he scanned the road but saw nothing unusual.

"Stay on it," he told Bishop.

Hawke set up both of the Satcom modules. The transmitter dish was pointed at the black sky and already tracking the path of the Magnus SIGINT satellite in high earth orbit. The CPU of the rig was flashing data on frequency, bandwidth and other pertinent technical matters.

Seconds later Hammerhead's telemetry was being absorbed and simultaneously transmitted via a full duplex linkage to the NSA listening post codenamed Playboy.

"Say your situation," the radio officer asked from his console at the NSA post as Playboy copied the field team's transmission.

"We're thirty klicks outside target designator Oxbow," Hawke replied while consulting the digital readout of his hand-held Magellan GPS.

He gave the coordinates for the extraction site. "Extraction will be hot," he added, and repeated the statement.

"I copy that, Hammerhead," the Playboy radio officer said. "They're on their way at this moment."

Hawke didn't need to inform Slater of the results of the transmission because the SLAM commander was crouching right beside him. Slater reloaded his weapon and rejoined Bishop.

"Trouble, boss," Bishop said.

Slater saw what it was.

There were headlights in the distance.

ANTICIPATING having to work under a slim lead time to reach the site for the scheduled extraction, the Pave Low chopper was already waiting just off the Turkish coast.

Now the pilot received the confirm and the coordinates of the pickup site, in addition to the information that the extraction would be hot. The pilot informed his crew of these specifics. The door gunners, already behind their weapons, put the GE Miniguns through final checks, ensuring that the feed lines from the ammo hoppers were free of impediments and that the guns' electrical systems were working correctly.

As the Pave Low's FLIR guidance system kept it pointed in the direction of the coordinates that the copilot had logged in to the chopper's fly-by-wire navigational system, other preparations were being made on board the Navy frigate *Southampton*.

At his station below decks, the frigate's battle-systems officer conducted a final status check and awaited launch confirmation from the skipper.

These orders came moments later, and the battle-systems officer enabled the final countdown sequence.

When the countdown zeroed out finally, the Tomahawk missile that had been computer programmed with the coordinates of the poppy field flamed on. The round whooshed from its launch container, arcing into the night. Shortly after launch, the booster stage separated from the warhead and the chemical rockets flamed on, stabilized by the sophisticated guidance package in the Tomahawk's nose.

The round's estimated time of arrival on target would be some fourteen minutes. At that point it would achieve a confirm and detonate with catastrophic consequences for those at whom it was aimed.

22

Slater instructed Bishop and Hawke to set up an L-shaped ambush to take out the armored vehicle approaching fast along the muddy mountain road.

Positioning Hawke with the final LAW AT-4 launcher in shoulder-fire position at the place where the road elbowed along the flanks of the granite outcropping, Slater positioned Bishop at the point of the ambush.

Slater was preparing to strike at the end of the ambush. His role would be to deliver the coup de grace to any survivors.

Within seconds the pursuit vehicle appeared. Probably of local construction, it was a fast attack vehicle of the Vickers Valkyr or Thyssen-Henschel TPz Fuchs configuration equipped with a pintle-mounted .50-caliber Browning machine gun.

Slater knew it as a type that would have an armored floor in addition to its shrapnel-resistant chassis as a defense against land mines. These factors alone did not necessarily make it impervious to coordinated time-on-target fire and would not stop a shaped charge, such as that produced by the AT-4's warhead, at close range.

Through night-vision-capable thirty-power Bushnells, Slater watched the eyes of the men in the cab of the armored fighting vehicle. Their gaze was directed straight ahead. Obviously they were oblivious to the presence of the commandos lying in wait behind the rock outcropping.

"Get ready," Hawke and Slater heard Bishop's tense voice say in the earbuds of their AN/PRC comsets as the truck approached.

Bishop opened up right on the money, tracking just ahead of the vehicle through the MG's unprotected sights as he lay prone on the muddy ground. Propped on its bipod legs, the M-60E3 began chattering with a trigger pull as cycling tracers rotored through the icy cold rain. A luminous flail of green dashes lashed out through the night as low-trajectory fire raked the target vehicle.

Striking the FAV broadside, the 7.62 mm bullets punched into the desert-camo-pattern hull armor as the war wagon neared the bend in the road.

The heavy vehicle was still moving as the gunner on top whipped the .50-caliber heavy machine gun around to train it on the source of the muzzle-flash. A moment later the big Browning was thudding away in a deep basso, cycling out its ammo at a slower rate than the higher-pitched Maremont, the rounds crisscrossing as they intersected in mid-course.

But the outcropping came between Bishop and the FAV's top gunner in a matter of pulse beats, and the .50-caliber fire ceased as the vehicle-mounted shooter lost visual contact.

Bishop's fire had dented the vehicle's armor plate, but the NATO-caliber rounds penetrated only sporadically. Nevertheless, the vehicle was softened up for Hawke, who, positioned at the L-shaped ambush site, trained the AT-4's sights on the front of the car as it careered into view.

With a fast calculation of windage, Hawke triggered the round.

With a whoosh of back blast as the round exited the pipe, the LAW's high-explosive warhead streaked through the night and struck the armored car broadside.

The warhead's conical-shaped charge deformed on detonation into a jet of semimolten steel and superheated gases. The lethal jet penetrated the side of the vehicle and the tough outer skin of riveted metal plates. Scything shrapnel and the overpressure caused by concussive blast combined with devastating effect.

Even before the razor-sharp fragments of disintegrating steel could rip into the lungs and other internal organs of the men inside, the FAV ruptured due to the extreme heat and overpressure. Its occupants died bleeding and screaming inside the vehicular death trap.

The vehicle's fuel tanks were next to go. Glowing red hot, the metal containers ignited the high-octane mixture within. Despite the fact that the tanks were protected by extra armor and sealed off with chemical additives the fuel tank went up in a violent explosion. Parts of the rear end of the car shot skyward amid gouts of towering flame.

Still the armored vehicle careered about as momentum catapulted it forward.

Slater was waiting for it at the end of its run, pumping glowing green 7.62 mm tracers into the vehicle as it stopped entirely and was consumed by another explosion.

"Hustle!" Slater yelled as Hawke flung the empty LAW casing to the ground and raced toward the truck. Hawke got behind the wheel, and Slater and Bishop rode shotgun as before with freshly reloaded M-60E3s.

Hard driving soon brought them to the extraction site indicated by the Magellan GPS units they carried.

The flat stretch of semiarid desert was open to the rainy night sky. Slater told Hawke to park the truck in the middle of the road.

He used the remainder of their explosives to mine the heavy truck with satchel charges that were linked to a remote fire-control unit he carried.

Within a matter of minutes the strike team heard the steady *thuk-a-thuk* of the Pave Low's powerful rotor blades churning the thin highland air. They saw the big chopper occult the stars as the ship appeared above the line of mountains to the north-west.

There was also more trouble on its way in the form of another vehicle coming up fast on the road toward their position.

Slater scrambled into position behind the rocks and initialized the hand-held infrared strobe unit that would mark the extraction site for the Pave Low's crew.

The chopper was almost overhead as the threat vehicle drew near. Heavy-caliber automatic fire flashed from the machine gun at its rear. Then came the sound of ratcheting gunfire and the whining of ricochets as the steel-jacketed bullets struck rock and fragmented off.

Slater hit the central button on the remote fire-control unit.

Mined with C-4 explosive charges, the heavy truck astride the road promptly blew up. Flames rose in a fireball from the exploding transport and forced the men in the pursuit vehicle to pull to a short stop or go careering into the wall of incinerating wreckage thrown up in their path.

The door gunners posted within the chopper went into action as the big helicopter swung toward the commandos.

They trained the GE Miniguns on the mercs who were spilling out of the stalled vehicle. The mercs in turn were firing their AKs up at the chopper. The man behind the .50-caliber gun swung the pintle-mounted weapon around and pointed it at the chopper on its heavy gimbals.

The effect of the cycling fire of the Miniguns was awesome to behold as they lashed down on the stunned mercs on the road. The MGs' multiple barrels, spitting out 7.62 mm bullets at a velocity of fifteen thousand rounds per minute, created a punching awl of incandescent steel.

The vortex of death struck fear into the hearts of the shooters before they were ultimately mowed down.

The pilot brought the big Pave Low to within a half meter of the ground, and Slater, Hawke and Bishop hustled toward its open rear hatch. They raced up the shallow incline and were inside the cabin as the chopper lifted up into the sky and rose to its "sagebrushing" altitude of sixty to seventy meters.

Below them, the still-burning wreckage of the heavy truck lit up the survivors of the brief though violent shootout in eerily flickering firelight. Those men who had not been killed by the Minigun fire were shooting Avtomats up at the chopper. The Pave Low was soon out of range of the assault weapons, though, and the stragglers ceased firing as it disappeared.

Within minutes the Pave Low was passing over the hilltop ruins where fires were still burning in the aftermath of SLAM's assault.

After it passed, the pilot saw the telltale luminous contrail of an incoming missile whose track was only a few meters below the MH-53J.

Although it was the Tomahawk round launched from the frigate *Southampton* and not directed at himself, his crew or the commandos under his care, the pilot knew that the risks were still great.

The blast from the special warhead could cause his chopper severe damage if he was not far enough away from its lethal radius in time.

Having been guided to the Turkish coast by its inertial navigation system, the incoming Tomahawk round passed the helicopter as it vectored in on its target on the low-trajectory, radar-evading flight path.

By now the missile had reached the point at which its terrain contour matching, or TERCOM, memory map was enabled, comparing an electronic grid of squares with the terrain below in order to keep the round on track.

When the Tomahawk was within forty meters of its target zone, its digital scene-matching correlator chipset came on-line. DSMAC activated the missile's look-down image-intensifying video camera and illuminated the ground with an IR strobe.

Matching the image of the poppy field to the image of light and dark grids stored in its DSMAC map, the Tomahawk went into its final detonation fusing sequence. Climbing again, the missile round detonated. A blinding flash was followed by a concussive thunderclap that had all the force of a miniature nuke.

Although the term *unconventional* was only used by the military to denote nuclear capability, there was nothing conventional about the warhead in a literal sense.

The warhead was a fuel-air explosive. Detonating as an airburst at some sixty meters, the FAE spawned a fireball that quickly grew to encompass the entire radius of the poppy field. In the aftermath of the blast, nothing would remain of the field but a gigantic shell crater over ninety meters in circumference.

Flying at the extreme edge of the blast zone, the Pave Low was nevertheless buffeted severely as the shock wave reached it.

Slater watched the horizon flicker with hellfire as the sudden, violent turbulence passed moments later. Like everyone else on board, the SLAM commando was glad he wasn't anywhere on the ground when that sucker had hit.

PART THREE:

Push the Envelope

23

A few minutes before Delta flight 798, which was scheduled to depart Frankfurt International Airport for a nonstop flight to Logan International in Boston, began boarding passengers, a traveler with a blue nylon barrel bag stopped for a drink at the Hofbrau Haus near the flight's departure lounge.

Standing at the edge of the bar, the passenger set down the barrel bag at his feet and caught the bartender's alert eye.

"A schnapps, please," he said in German.

"Right away, sir," the bartender replied in the same language.

"And have you got any matches?" the passenger continued. "I seem to have run out."

"Compliments of the house, sir," the bartender said, sliding two matchbooks across at the passenger, completing the recognition sequence.

Apart from his skills at mixology, the bartender was a member of the Fighting Communist Cells, a group counting Iran as its principal funding agency.

The bartender had already received his instructions and knew what to do when the recognition sequence was satisfactorily completed.

A few minutes later the passenger rose upon hearing the announcement that his flight was preparing to board. When he left, it was with a barrel bag identical in appearance to the one he had set down on the floor on coming into the Hofbrau Haus.

But appearances were in this case deceiving. The barrel bag that the airline passenger had brought into the bar and which the bartender had now stowed behind it, contained balled sheets of the *Frankfurter Zeitung*.

The much heavier bag that the flier carried out of the Hofbrau Haus contained three Army Universal Guns, better known as AUGs. In addition to the compact yet formidable 5.56 mm assault weapons, the barrel bag contained several hundred rounds of the hardball SS109 ammo. It also contained several APERS grenades, complete with pull-string attachments to permit remote detonation or to set up explosive booby traps.

Soon the passenger was shuffling toward the departure gate with his carryon bag amid a line of passengers whose seats bore even numbers like his own. Although he spoke to no one and ostensibly had no discernible acquaintances in line, two men who had already boarded flight 798 knew the flier quite well. They and he were members of the terrorist group Hezbollah and had trained together in Iran and Libya.

They were about to carry out a mission that they had long trained for and awaited with a mixture of rapture and dread. They were filled with holy awe at the prospect of becoming martyred heroes to the great revolutionary cause.

Only a flick of the eyes indicated recognition by the first two of the third man carrying the bag of weapons as he took his seat in front of them. They did not move as he slid the blue nylon barrel bag beneath his seat.

They would act only when he would turn to them and utter: "Al Khoul." This was the leader's code name. He gave the orders, and "Jihad" and "Baraka" would obey them with their lives.

The moment to act came as Al Khoul saw the captain enter the plane, exchange words with two female flight attendants near the forward boarding hatch and go into the cockpit.

One of the flight attendants then proceeded to dog down the hatch. When it had closed, Al Khoul turned to the two men in back and nodded.

Within minutes, the AUGs were in their hands, black ski masks were pulled tautly over their faces and they were spreading out through the cockpit as they had done countless times during exercises in the mock-ups of commercial airline interiors in terrorist training grounds in Iran.

Gesturing for the stunned flight attendants to move aside, Al Khoul rapped on the cockpit door. Entering the cockpit, he pointed the AUG at the two uniformed pilots who sat stunned behind the control panel.

"This plane is being commandeered in the name of the Iranian Party of God," he announced loudly. "You are to follow my instructions to the letter if you value your lives and the lives of your crew and passengers."

IT WAS five p.m. in Frankfurt when the hijacking took place. It took more than an hour for the first news reports of the hijacking to be broadcast out of Germany. The reason behind this was the automatic lid placed on all reports of terrorist acts as per Germany's antiterrorist policy.

By the time the first confirmed reports of the terrorist hijacking reached Washington, it was a little past midnight, local time.

The report required an additional hour of thorough analysis and vetting until the President was finally awakened shortly after one a.m. He was told the news and advised that a considerable number of the one hundred forty-seven passengers were American citizens.

The caller was the director of the Central Intelligence Agency. As he spoke to the President he was on his way to the CIA's Langley headquarters via the Washington beltway.

Beside him a portable cellular fax machine was spitting out a stream of situation updates from Agency forward observers across the globe.

"How bad does it look, Jim?" the President asked James P. Blocker, who could hear the muzziness in the CinC's voice.

"Too early to tell," the DCI replied over the secure phone, "but I won't pull any punches. It doesn't look to be a cakewalk."

"Any preliminary Intelligence as to the reason behind it? The group or groups responsible?"

"That we're getting an early fix on," the DCI said even as he scanned the most recent fax spit out by the portable machine. "We think it's Hezbollah, and I'm sorry to say that the hijacking doesn't come as a shock."

"You mean in light of the recent intelligence about Iran's regional ambitions?" the President queried.

"That's correct," the DCI returned.

"Carry on, Jim," the President told the director. "And keep me posted."

"Will do," the DCI said as he signed off and placed the phone down on the seat beside him.

As he scanned the faxes, rechecking and sifting through the welter of details the various agents in place were reporting, it was clear to him that the timing of the hijacking dovetailed with the operation against the Iran-funded French Connection resurgence.

Iran, by way of Hezbollah, was sending the United States a message. But the DCI had a message of his own to send them, one in a language he knew they would understand.

24

The Lockheed C-130 Hercules four-engine multipurpose transport aircraft stood warming up on the floodlit runway. Its immense rear hatchway was open, exposing the cavernous lighted interior.

The C-130 was an aircraft designed to haul anywhere between five and six thousand kilos of military payload across a distance of some twenty-five hundred nautical miles—considerably more with AAR, air-to-air refueling. Yet its short takeoff and landing, or STOL, capability meant it could also use unprepped airfields in combat situations.

The globe-straddling turboprop aircraft had been one of America's critical pieces of machinery in effecting the massive strategic airlift that had worked the miracle of the Desert Shield buildup in the Arabian desert. It had helped to give the United States the equivalent of seven league boots in the race to beat Saddam to the punch.

The time was 0345 hours, and the night sky over Riyadh was a moonless black inverted bowl flecked with diamond-faceted stars.

Approaching the C-130 along the tarmac apron of the Saudi air base were three men in paramilitary fatigues, regulation jump boots and full field kit including tactical vests and rucksack.

Deal Slater, Mason Hawke and Eddie Bishop had been briefed by Jack Callixto, their liaison officer, on the specifics of the mission, as well as its underlying logistical considerations.

At that moment, each member of SLAM knew, the hijacked Delta Airline passenger jet sat immobilized on the tarmac of Frankfurt International Airport, the one hundred forty-seven passengers still on board being held at gunpoint by a group of ski-masked terrorists.

It was some twelve hours since the hijacking had begun and the demands of the hijackers been broadcast to a dumbstruck world by global news media. As was generally the case in such matters, the demands of the hijackers came in two editions: one for public and media consumption, the other—and generally the true demands—for the eyes and ears of Intelligence operatives.

To the reporters of CNN and the other news media, the hijackers represented themselves as a Hezbollah splinter group demanding that American security forces withdraw from the Middle East.

To the Intelligence community, however, the demands were a great deal more specific. In this case it was made clear that the covert paramilitary strikes launched recently against drug cartel bases in France, in Mediterranean waters and finally in southern Turkey, had prompted the hijacking of the commercial jetliner.

Furthermore, the secret cable traffic made it clear that the hijacking would be the first of many such terrorist acts against Americans and their allies. It would be but the springboard to a renewed terror campaign that would go on as long as the United States continued to interfere in Iran's plans.

These threats originated at the highest levels of the Iranian parliament. They included blackmail threats to expose highly damaging secrets, which Hezbollah learned through its lengthy interrogation under torture of CIA station chief William Buckley, as well as further data pertaining to the arms-for-hostages deals of the secret Iran-Contra negotiations.

However, at a series of meetings both open and covert, including an emergency session of the National Security Council only a few hours before, it was deemed that no threat facing both America and the current presidential administration had more potentially severe repercussions then failing to act decisively in the face of the new Hezbollah terror initiative.

While spin control was possible in the wake of Iranian Intelligence leaks, it would prove disastrous for a post-gulf-war America to be seen to knuckle under again to terrorist fanatics as it was seen to do during the Carter years.

The war on drugs had finally come up against the underlying reality of the drug supply's genesis: the fact that governments were always major players. But the architects of the drug war had foreseen this contingency and planned for it all along. Force would be met with force.

Saddam had finally taught America that only the hand that wielded the sword with courage and skill could hold aloft the olive branch of peace to a merciless enemy.

The SLAM team's newest mission objective was a preemptive strike against the Iranians who had sent out the Hezbollah group. Slater and his crew understood that it flowed naturally from their dominant strategy of closing down the Istanbul-to-Marseilles heroin pipeline before it could become entrenched.

This they had done but not completely.

Behind the pipeline stood the Iranians, whose original objectives were unchanged. The Iranians wanted to purchase the four essential ingredients on the shopping list of any nation that wanted to join the nuclear club: basic technology, brainpower, component parts and fissionable fuel.

So far, the Iranians had used revenues from the heroin pipeline to add to their supply of the first three ingredients, including ultrahard maraging steel, vital for both fuel processing and bomb construction.

The fourth ingredient, fissionable fuel of a grade high enough to process into nuclear bomb cores, was already in the early stages of production at the secret nuclear-weapons facility located in the Iranian desert and given the code name "Omar-7."

The Omar-7 facility had been constructed by a cooperative of French, German and American firms during the period when the gulf war had provided a convenient smoke screen for the arrival of components critical to the manufacture of weapons-grade plutonium—gas centrifuges.

While Iraq was the focus of controversy and Intelligence analysis regarding its own nuclear weapons aspirations, the Iranians had seen their chance to act. Although international firms openly disclaimed involvement with Saddam's weapons program, they were taking down payments from the Iranians for high-tech components that were forbidden to Saddam.

In the minds of powerful corporate officials faced with the prospect of multimillion dollar losses, greed had overcome conscience.

At Omar-7 preliminary steps were under way to convert uranium into its fissionable counterpart, plutonium 238. The naturally occurring radioactive element may be enriched by several means. In the case of Iran, gas centrifuging was the process being used.

Although this process was among the most advanced, the CIA's analysis judged the Iranians as having enough fissionable material to put together a crude though functional bomb within months.

SLAM's mission was not only to take out Omar-7 but to take it out in a way consonant with coalition strike doctrine in the gulf war. Omar-7 was to be obliterated by a method that would tell the Iranians in no uncertain terms that they would not prevail in their aim of becoming a nuclear power.

It was hoped that a successful strike by SLAM would, in the first place, curtail the production of the Iranian bomb. In the second place, it would demonstrate that there was no payoff in continuing to rely on drug revenues to fund the project.

A third objective would be achieved by itself: the Iranians would desert the terrorists holding flight 798 on the ground and the Germans, with a little help from Delta Force, would take care of the rest.

25

Flying from Riyadh on a northeasterly course vector, the C-130 Hercules crossed the Persian Gulf at wave-scudding altitude. A few minutes later the plane was passing over dry land again and was inside Iranian territory.

In the cockpit the pilot consulted the navigator monitoring the plane's AN-APQ-175 radar navigation system and confirmed their course heading against the terrain-mapping system computer.

The C-130's radar-systems operator scanned the banks of threat-recognition radars. Linked to computers, those devices analyzed the backscatter and could give advance warning of threats. The radar operator was gratified that the banks of digitized screens all continued to indicate that no hostile aircraft had detected the aircraft. He hoped that their luck continued to hold.

As lacking in armament as it was gigantic in size, the C-130 would have zero chance against Iranian fighters should any be scrambled to intercept and shoot it down. Its crew's hope of getting to their objective and returning safely to base lay solely in the aircraft's ability to evade radar detection.

Like the pilot, navigator and radar operator, another key member of the C-130's flight crew, the mission's loadmaster, was also carrying out his part of the assignment.

To the loadmaster fell the responsibility of ensuring that the men and matériel that the C-130 hauled across the skies got placed accurately and safely at their objective.

In this case, that meant not only seeing that the three snake eaters on board made their jumps at the right time and landed in one piece, but that the specially requisitioned military materials that went into the DZ with them also got where they were supposed to, also in one piece.

When the navigator reported via the internal commo that some twenty minutes remained till ETA, the loadmaster ran a final check on the hardware that was secured to its special low-altitude parachute extraction system—LAPES—pallets on the floor.

First among these was a fast-attack vehicle, or FAV. The loadmaster was familiar with dropping this type of military load. He had done so on many occasions during the war in the gulf.

The small vehicle looked a great deal like a dune buggy, but there the resemblance began and ended.

No dune buggy was equipped with the .50-caliber H-Bar Barret machine gun at the rear, nor the two M-60s pointing frontward.

Nor would you be likely to find the same type of specially constructed General Motors engine inside the tube chassis of a buggy on the dunes along the Atlantic Coast or the Southwest. This particular engine was highly resistant to the presence in valves, pistons and other critical components, of the microfine particles of desert grit that made up the sands of the Middle Eastern deserts.

The loadmaster knew that the Special Forces guys respected the capabilities of the FAVs and knew that this one was newly constructed and checked out sixteen ways from Sunday. Now the loadmaster himself conducted one of his own many checks, ensuring that the parachute lines were unfouled and that the chutes would open at the optimum angle once the pallet was in free-fall.

There was one other item of matériel that was going down with the FAV for use by the snake eaters. The loadmaster didn't like the looks of it. According to the computer manifest he'd scanned during the loading phase, the item was a "special munition." The label was repeated on markings on the specially cushioned foam cocoon that encased it as it rested on the C-130's deck.

A specialist in the nomenclature by which the U.S. military defined its bewildering array of field matériel, the loadmaster knew all about "special munitions," although he had personally never handled such a load himself.

He knew that in U.S. military usage, the word *special* when used in connection with *explosives* referred to one type and one alone: nuclear. The loadmaster paid this second item the respect he felt it was due and hoped that he'd be far away when it went off.

While the loadmaster checked the LAPES pallets, the three men he considered snake eaters were busy with pre-drop checks of their own. Slater and his crew had also been advised by the aircraft's navigator over the cockpit-to-cabin intercom that they were twenty minutes from the DZ and were running through final weapons and equipment checks.

In addition, the members of the SLAM team each pitched in to apply the tiger stripes of black and green nonreflective camo paint to each other's face.

Before long the C-130 had come within ten minutes of its mission objective. Linked by a global positioning system to a phased array of orbiting Navstar geosatellites, the navigator relied on state-of-the-art electronics to guide the craft to the unmarked drop zone.

The computer-driven radar screens continued to show no sign that the transport aircraft was in the sights of the Iranians, while the pilot's scopes showed that the terrain below held no unanticipated obstacles.

In the cargo bay, Slater, Hawke and Bishop fastened their chute belts and, under the observation of the loadmaster, turned toward the rearward hatch.

Because of the requirement that the C-130 fly in under the radar curtain and because the drop zone was unmarked, a HALO, or high-altitude, low-opening parachute, drop would not be carried out. Such drops were conducted from altitudes of approximately ten thousand meters, and the plane was flying far too low for this to be practical.

Instead, a low-altitude, low-opening drop would be conducted. This type of drop was generally made from the vicinity of three hundred meters, using the more conventionally shaped T-1 parachutes as opposed to the parafoils generally associated with HALO drops.

The SLAM team hooked the static lines of their T-1 parachutes to the overhead cable that ran along the length of the aircraft and gathered up the slack. At the five-minute warning, the strike team checked their static lines, ensuring that the snap hooks were correctly attached to the overhead cable, signaling that all was in order with a tap on the shoulder of the man to the front.

When the aircraft was in position over the DZ, the pilot turned on the green light above the hatch, signaling to the loadmaster and his commando "guests" that the time for the drop had arrived. He then put the Hercules into a tight turn and re-crossed the drop zone.

Slater went first at the loadmaster's thumbs-up, his main chute blossoming open approximately four seconds after he went into free-fall. Hawke followed one second later, with Bishop a second later as the last man out of the plane.

The loadmaster watched the three T-1 chutes open flawlessly, the black nylon circles barely discernable against the darkness of night sky and shadow-shrouded sand. Beneath the first black canopy he could see Slater pull on his risers to compensate for a sudden updraft. He touched down seconds later, collapsing onto his side and cushioning the shock of landing with thighs and shoulders.

From a sitting position he released the riser from his shoulder to spill air from the canopy, then hit the three quick-release catches on the harness, freeing himself from the chute.

The process was repeated two more times, and minutes later the loadmaster's practiced eyes saw the three men who had hit the ground digging holes to bury their chutes.

The loadmaster signaled the cockpit that the three snake eaters were on the ground.

"They're down," the loadmaster said to the pilot. "Standing by to begin the LAPES drop."

"That's affirm," the voice replied.

The pilot banked the C-130 hard to bring it full around in a tight circle. At the same time he began to descend from the three-hundred-meter altitude at which the personnel had parachuted out to fly only a few meters off the desert floor.

By this time the loadmaster had lowered the rear hatchway and deployed the extraction parachute of the first palletized drop load. Caught by the wind, the extraction chute blossomed, pulling out the main chute from the rear of the plane and taking the palletized cargo with it.

FIRST UP AFTER BURYING his chute in the sandy crust of the Iranian desert, Eddie Bishop watched the two black parachutes blossom open a few hundred meters from the rear hatchway of the orbiting C-130.

The pallet at the end of the first chute contained the FAV. It hit the ground only about forty meters from his position.

Following close behind was the SADM, the special atomic demolition munition, encased in its protective shock-proof cocoon. It would be Bishop's responsibility to unload and carry the 4.5-kiloton nuclear device to the mission strike objective.

OVERHEAD, the rear hatchway of the C-130 was already closing up as the Hercules completed its LAPES drop, climbed and prepared to exit the drop zone.

Receiving a visual confirm that the troops and matériel had all been placed in the drop zone safely, the loadmaster picked up the mike beside him and transmitted that information to the pilot, who advised him that he copied that and thanked him for a job well done.

The pilot punched in a new course heading, one that would take the C-130 back to Riyadh by a slightly different route. He put the Hercules into a turn that would point its nose to the southwest.

With his hands on the controls of the big transport plane, the pilot was feeling a slight untightening at the pit of his stomach at the prospect of completing the dangerous mission's first leg.

But the radar operator had no hands-on control over anything and so could not avail himself of the illusion of semisafety that the pilot could. He continued to scan his scopes and hoped for the best. The nature of his job made it clear to him that it would only be over when it was over and not a single second before.

26

While Iranian ground radar along the western border did not detect the C-130 as it flew a low-trajectory course above the desert floor, it was visible to anyone who happened to be looking up at the right time.

Such was the case as the Hercules transport neared the Persian Gulf, roughly twenty-five kilometers from friendly airspace.

The bedouin was a goatherd who lived in a stone shack just north of Bandar 'Abbas.

He had retired hours earlier and had been sleeping the deep, dreamless sleep that only those who toil from sunup to sundown can know when he was awakened by a sound the likes of which he had never heard before.

The sound seemed to fill the crudely built stone hut as though it were a living presence. It was a roaring sound, louder and deeper than that he imagined a thousand lions capable of producing if they all roared at once. And the sound seemed to make the walls vibrate as it neared the hut.

Dressed in his nightshirt, the old goatherd hastened to the door of his hut and looked around. In the sky overhead he saw the source of the noise that had awakened him from his well-earned slumber and his mouth hung agape.

The plane seemed to be enormous. Its wings seemed to enfold the night sky, and its belly was of gigantic proportions to match them.

The old man's perception of the great size of the plane was enhanced by the fact that it was flying only a few feet over the roof of the goatherd's shack, and for an instant the old man was fearful that it was about to crash.

If it exploded nearby, he might be killed.

In a matter of seconds, the plane passed completely overhead. Seeing that it was not going to crash—at least near his house—the shepherd was somewhat relieved.

As the roar of the turboprop engines faded and the C-130 vanished into a black dot on the horizon, the goatherd's fear left him entirely, and something else took root in its place.

The old man had lived almost seventy years as a bedouin Arab among Persians who did not hold his kind in high esteem. In that time he had learned that there are times to hold one's silence and times to speak out. This time his sense of self-preservation told him that he should speak out.

There was a police barracks not far away in Bandar 'Abbas where he could report the strange plane he had seen. If he made the report, he could not be held accountable later on, in the event anything unfortunate happened. Yes, he decided, that was what he would do.

In the morning he would go to the police barracks at Bandar 'Abbas and report what he had seen and what he had heard.

But now his fatigue was beginning to come back to him again. With a yawn, the old goatherd turned, went back into his shack and was soon fast asleep, not to be awakened until the rising of the sun.

AFTER THE C-130 DEPARTED from the drop zone, SLAM broke down the containerized packaging in which the specialized matériel had been transported. Then they buried every scrap of evidence that might call attention to their presence.

While Slater stood scout duty, Bishop and Hawke scoured every inch of the drop area for the telltale presence of any bit of foreign matter, no matter how insignificant. Because the circumference of the drop zone was some sixty meters in its entirety, this was no small feat. Nevertheless, it had to be done, however difficult and time-consuming.

When the drop zone was finally secured, the SLAM team boarded the fast-attack vehicle and drove from the area to their intermediate objective. Code-named Overlook, this objective was a dry wadi some one hundred ten klicks from their present position.

Barring any unforeseen contingencies, the SLAM team would reach Overlook shortly before daybreak. Once in place, they would secure the FAV beneath camouflage tarp and take up alternate recon and rest duties for the duration of the day. Because all movement would be confined to the hours of darkness between sunset and sunrise, the SLAM team would stay at Overlook until well after nightfall.

When the desert had cooled enough to make undetected travel easier, they would remount the FAV and proceed to their second objective, a recon position just outside the Omar-7 nuclear weapons facility. Once having reached this objective, they would subject the strike perimeter to a final recon, receive a go/no-go via Satcom transmission from Playboy and take it from there, depending on their final instructions.

Slater, at the wheel of the FAV, pointed the big-wheeled sand vehicle toward Wadi Qasam, determining his course via hand-held global positioning unit. He did not know that the pressure to mount the strike was building. In Frankfurt, Germany, it was late in the afternoon and on the tarmac apron of Frankfurt International, another American citizen had been shot by the Hezbollah terrorists and dumped onto the blacktop before the world media.

The mission clock was ticking.

27

GPS-based land navigation permitted SLAM to roll across the Iranian desert toward Wadi Qasam without unnecessary delay. The way points at Tel Erand and Tel Bindar were reached on schedule, and in both places the team paused only long enough to conduct a recon.

An hour before daybreak of strike day one, Slater and his crew were bunkered in at Overlook with camo netting pulled across the dry hole in the desert ground.

With the sunrise came the heat, which increased steadily until the mean temperature as measured by SLAM's equipment rose to some one hundred ten degrees Fahrenheit.

Throughout the day the three strikers swapped sack time and watch duty, reenacting the pattern of activity that was standard procedure on their previous missions.

It was early in the afternoon of strike day one when Hawke, who was taking the second watch, spotted something moving on the far horizon.

Through the shimmering curtain of thermal distortion brought about by the sun's heat reflected from the baking sands, it was at first difficult to pinpoint the nature of the activity.

At first he thought it might be "Bob" out there, a bedouin caravan or something on that order, but his gut told him it wasn't. In time Hawke realized that his initial suspicions were confirmed: he was looking at a mechanized patrol column.

Slater had issued instructions to awaken him if anything of this nature was detected, but in any case Hawke or Bishop would require no special instructions to relay such findings to their team leader.

Slater was up within seconds and peering through the precision-ground lenses of the Bushnell field glasses at the column, which was now far more easily recognizable, even through heat distortion, as it drew nearer their position.

The mechanized patrol appeared to be comprised of an armored personnel carrier and two fast scout vehicles. All of them were recognizable as Egyptian-manufactured copies of European designs. The vehicles were painted in a dun desert camo pattern and bore the crescent and sword that marked them as belonging to the Iranian Pasdaran or Revolutionary Guard Corps.

Slater could see the black snouts of .50-caliber machine guns bristling from all three vehicles, which, as he watched, turned from their original broadside position to move headlong in their direction. By now the patrol was less than a dozen kilometers away.

Continuing his recon, Slater watched as the patrol leader raised his arm and signaled the other two vehicles to stop by fanning it briskly from side to side. Through his field glasses he could see the Iranian soldier raise a pair of field glasses and scan ahead and to his flanks.

"How's it look?" asked Bishop, who by now had joined Slater and Hawke near the edge of the camouflaged wadi, all three of them wearing ghillie cover.

"Not too damned good," Slater replied. "It looks like they're looking for something or somebody. Maybe it's us and maybe not."

Slater crunched the numbers as he continued to watch the behavior of the column commander, who now put away his field glasses and signaled the column forward again.

If the op had in fact been compromised somehow and they were being hunted by the Iranians, then there would be no possibility of making a run for it before the patrol reached their position. On the other hand, the patrol might not be looking for them at all and might be simply engaging in a routine exercise.

The camouflage netting that concealed their position and the FAV was of sophisticated design and resistant to thermal-imaging technologies, as well as to conventional visual detection. If the patrol did not come too close, then they might well pass by entirely.

But after a little while it became apparent to Slater that the Iranians were heading directly for the wadi.

At the rate they were traveling, Slater estimated that there was no more than a few minutes lead time.

Putting aside the Bushnells, Slater hefted the Maremont MG and placed it in the sand on its bipod legs, instructing Hawke and Bishop to do the same with their .50-caliber Barrets, specially outfitted to take ammo from high-capacity feed boxes.

His strategy was to open up with the heavy-caliber automatic weapons and throw saturation fire at the patrol before they could react. With any luck, SLAM might be able to pound them down before the APC put a mortar round right in the middle of their position.

SLAM watched the patrol come close enough to hear the grinding and clanking of the transmissions of the vehicles, smell the odors of engine exhaust and hear the shouts of the Iranians who manned the column.

Slater tightened his grip on the trigger of the Maremont, telling Hawke and Bishop to hold their fire until he signaled to open up with coordinated bursts. But then something happened to change the entire nature of the confrontation.

The Iranian patrol was still rolling forward, only a few meters from the wadi, when completely without warning, the sky to the east began to darken. Within a matter of seconds a deep shadow had spread across the landscape, accompanied by a strange whining sound that steadily and rapidly built into an unearthly banshee howl.

In seconds the sandstorm was completely on them. Fierce winds churned up a moving column of reddish brown dust that rose hundreds of meters into the air and moved across the landscape with the speed of a runaway locomotive. Dwarfing the power of any man-made weapon of war, the fierce storm engulfed both the Iranians and the U.S. commandos.

On the Iranian side, those inside the APC enjoyed the highest level of safety as the storm raced past. Those in the two open cars donned protective goggles and clung precariously to whatever handholds they could get on their vehicles as the storm roared past.

The Iranians knew the ways of the desert, however, and knew that the sandstorm would be as brief as it was ferocious.

It was over within minutes. The Iranians dug themselves out of the several meters of sand that had blown onto their vehicles, temporarily losing sight of the reports of enemy commandos in the area. This proved, very quickly, to be a terminally dangerous error in judgment for the Iranians.

Aided by some of the troops who had climbed out of the APC, the soldiers in the scout cars were breaking out shovels when the small nearby dunes of windblown sand deposited by the storm seemed to explode. Disoriented as they saw their comrades drop, the survivors of the burst were slow to grasp what was happening.

Slater, Hawke and Bishop had used the sandstorm to advantage.

They had left the concealed position in the wadi during the storm and crawled to positions abreast of the stalled patrol column. Hunkering down on the ground with their weapons pointed at the Iranians, SLAM allowed the windstorm to do the rest of the work for them.

In moments they were covered with the millions of fine particles of windblown sand.

The sand deposits dumped by the sudden storm covered them almost completely. The portions of their anatomy that protruded were also invisible, thanks to camouflage netting covering weapons barrels and the concealing properties of the desert BDUs they wore.

Now, with the storm past, the three strikers stood up, sand pouring from their BDUs as the two .50-caliber Barrets and Slater's 7.62 mm Maremont cycled out their obliterating rounds.

More of the Iranians went down as Slater lobbed a grenade into the open hatchway of the Iranian APC. The personnel carrier exploded, dark smoke billowing out of the hatchway as overpressure channeled the blast up through the topside opening in a column of smoke and flame.

He heard screams from inside the burning vehicle as Iranian troopers were being burned alive. Slater pulled a second grenade and threw it in. A second explosion fixed it so there were no more screams.

The silence was total only moments after the burst commenced.

All of the Iranians had been KIA'd.

The rest of the afternoon was spent in disposing of the remains of the column and in completely sanitizing the killing ground. Then SLAM moved on to its next and final objective.

28

With the charred and bullet-pocked hulks of the Iranian mechanized column buried in the wadi, and with the coming of darkness, SLAM prepared to move.

However, before they did, Mason Hawke, the strike team's technical specialist, transmitted a scheduled situation report via the Satcom communications rig.

During his transmission, Hawke informed Playboy of their engagement with the Iranian patrol. In addition, he requested another go/no-go confirm.

The go condition remained in force, but the strike team was apprised of the fact that a Keyhole 12 phased satellite array over the operations zone indicated that the patrol that SLAM had encountered was one of several scouring the desert. Apparently they were searching for them.

Hawke signed off and broke down the Satcom unit. With the confirm received, the team moved out and proceeded to their next mission objective.

In the light of the new Intelligence and the unit's recent brush with the Iranian patrol column, the team proceeded from Overlook to their final pre-strike recon point with a heightened sense of caution.

The Intel meant that the operation had been compromised; to what extent was not known. The best that could be hoped was that the opposition's knowledge of SLAM's mission was not great enough to affect the outcome or result in the killing or capture of the team itself.

ALL THREE SLAM team members wore AN/PVS night-vision goggles strapped across their cammied faces as they proceeded through the night across the trackless desert sands.

While Slater drove their commando vehicle, Hawke sat facing the rear of the FAV, his tactical-gloved hands grasping the .50 caliber Barret machine gun, his NVG-augmented eyes scanning the horizon for indications of ground- or air-delivered threats.

The heavy-barreled version of the standard Barret machine gun was mounted on a pintle stand and was fed from a high-capacity ammo box attached to the stand. The .50-caliber gun had a full three-hundred-sixty-degree arc of fire and was loaded with tracers every fourth round as had become standard procedure with SLAM in the field.

Bishop, up front beside Slater, retracted his Litton-made NVGs, scanning the terrain through a binocular night observation device, or NOD. Also manufactured by Litton, the M976 starlight scope incorporated the same GEN III antibloom technology as the NVGs, and could be used during night operations under all battle conditions.

The journey across the desert passed uneventfully throughout the first half of their estimated six hours of travel. Midway across their trek, Slater stopped the FAV so the team could conduct a scheduled position recon. This was fortunate because the team discovered another Iranian patrol not far away during their reconnaissance activities.

The terrain of the northeastern Iranian desert is not completely flat but is instead made up of vast stretches of often spectacular mountains and plateaus. These rock formations rival those of the American Southwest.

The FAV had stopped above a gradual descent in the terrain. Moving forward toward the edge of the high ground, Bishop looked down onto the low-lying country below. Peering through the NOD, he saw that an Iranian mechanized column was halted just below.

It appeared that the Iranians had stopped at a desert refueling station—there were nearly empty rubber fuel bladders near the column—and that the column was about to move out, proceeding in SLAM's direction.

Bishop had just enough time to signal to Slater—who was gassing up the FAV from its portable fuel stores—and Hawke, who was cleaning his weapon. The SLAM team immediately rolled the FAV into a position of concealment and deployed to ambush the patrol column. Barely were they in position, taking advantage of the cover of a sizable stone outcrop, than the Iranian column came rolling and clanking into view.

Slater opened fire with a LAW rocket while Hawke, from atop the FAV, poured .50-caliber fire at the column using the pintle-mounted Barret MG.

Bishop, spelling Slater, was behind the wheel of the fast moving vehicle as the Iranians opened fire. The highly mobile attack vehicle enabled them to evade the hostile fire as they sighted in on their quarry.

With the lead Iranian APC now in firing range, Slater cut loose with an AT-4 high-explosive warhead. As the portable launcher tube bucked on his shoulder, he felt the bird leave the pipe amid a backwash of acrid-smelling propellent smoke and hot exhaust.

Moments later the shaped charge was injecting a long spike of semimolten steel and shrapnel into the armored hull of the APC while blast effect took care of the rest.

The Iranian troops on board the two fast cars opened up with .50-caliber guns mounted on pintles at the rear of the vehicles, but the FAV was a lot more maneuverable than the heavier armored cars.

Bishop, behind the wheel, was able to dart in close, then pull out far again, always staying ahead of the tracking capabilities of the Iranians on board the war wagons, whose inexperience in high-mobility combat contributed to the speed of their destruction.

The final scout car went up as glowing green tracers from Hawke's blazing .50-caliber machine gun stitched out a line of hits along its flanks until glowing tracers punched one of the vehicle's weak spots near its rear end and penetrated its gas tank. The ensuing explosion lifted up the chassis of the staff car amid a spreading fireball that reared high into the night.

It looked like the cold-smoked column's destruction would bring an end to conflict, but a major problem appeared in the form of a helicopter that seemed to pop up out of nowhere, as if it had been hiding beneath the sands.

In truth, the chopper had been flying nap of the earth, hugging the contours of the rising and falling desert landscape to sneak up on the battle zone unseen and unheard above the din of war.

When it unmasked behind the high ridge of rocky boulders, the chopper was practically right on top of the fight that had just concluded.

The rocket impacted near the FAV, detonating with bright flashes and loud booms that shook the ground. The lightweight vehicle was nearly bowled over. Fortunately it was far enough from the missile warhead for SLAM to escape harm by moving fast.

Bishop's combat-honed reflexes reacted instantly. He veered the FAV on an evasive course while Hawke and Slater turned to meet the new threat.

Another rocket salvo was less effective still as SLAM got its bearings and launched an AT-4 warhead and withering salvos of .50-caliber Barret MG fire at the chopper.

But the chopper pilot was good and apparently determined to score a shutout.

He darted the steel dragonfly out of range of the strikes and was not hurt by the HEAT counterfire that SLAM had launched his way.

Had Slater been deploying Stingers, also included in field kit, the situation might have been different. But in the cramped confines of the FAV, it was impossible to deploy the heat-seeking antiaircraft weapon, which was significantly heavier and more unwieldy than the LAW design.

"Drop me off and run interference," Slater told Bishop, who flashed him the thumbs-up in response.

Slater unshipped the Stinger rig that the strike team had brought along just in case it met up with unfriendly helicopters. Now he had it deployed and nodded to Bishop as Bishop slowed the FAV and Slater jumped from the fast-moving vehicle.

Seeing the advanced-design man-portable armament Slater was packing, the chopper pilot veered toward the lone commando. But the pulsing fire from Hawke's rotoring Barret forced the chopper to turn its full attention to the nettlesome FAV, which moved across the desert floor like some sand viper squirting poison at the steel dragonfly in the night sky.

The chopper pilot swung low and brought his 20 mm Vulcan cannon into furious play. But by this time Slater had deployed a Stinger. He pointed the manpads weapon system at the chopper and got the chopper in his sights. A target lock was identified by a long beep-tone and Slater depressed the trigger-style firing stud of the fire-and-forget weapon.

The high-explosive, heat-seeking warhead tracked on the chopper. From the instant that the Stinger had acquired its target, the chopper was as good as killed. The round struck amidships, homing in on the heat of the engine exhaust. It went right down the pipe and exploded well inside the engine cowling where it could do maximum damage to the chopper and aircrew.

White-hot shrapnel sprayed the assets inside the chopper as the round blew. Close on the heels of the lethal splinter burst came a moving wall of broiling flame that melted the flesh from their bones and practically cooked the aircrew in their own blood.

They had almost enough time to scream as the fireball that was ripping apart the hull of the chopper tore their burning limbs off their flailing torsos.

From the ground, the SLAM shadow warriors watched the chopper become a blooming ball of incandescence as the round ripped through it.

Though blindingly intense, the fireball was brief in duration and lit up the desert in a strobing pattern that made the darkness of night appear as though it were high noon.

Soon Slater was throwing the spent though reusable Stinger launcher into the FAV as Bishop brought the vehicle around to retrieve him. There would be no time for sanitizing any of the kills.

There might not even be enough time for the strike team to make it to its final objective before SLAM had to contend with an even greater search party.

The op had been compromised. Now there was no question about it. In a world of uncertainties one fact was sure: it would not get any easier from here on out.

29

The desert was vast, and SLAM had little choice but to continue the mission much as originally conceived. An emergency extraction this deep in Iranian territory was possible, but the prospect of its happening was not likely due to a variety of logistical considerations.

The scale of distances in the desert worked in SLAM's favor. The Iranians might not understand the full extent of the threat facing them and they probably would not yet guess the true objective of the strike. The hunt for three men among thousands of square kilometers of open desert was like searching for the proverbial needle in the haystack.

Nevertheless, SLAM moved quickly and in a random fashion, pausing frequently to conduct area recons before resuming.

They moved through the night, putting as much distance between the scene of the ambush and firefight as they could before they reached their final recon point, code-named Whirlwind. They arrived before dawn of strike day two.

Although Slater and his crew could not know it, Slater's guess about the opposition's Intel on their situation had been borne out by events.

The Iranians did not in fact know their whereabouts and had not received accurate reports from the field, only garbled information. The enemy would be surprised to know that an American commando team carrying a nuclear device was headed toward Omar-7 intent on destroying the nuclear facility.

SLAM PUSHED on steadily through the night, and reached their final objective well ahead of schedule.

The first thing that the team did was to stash the FAV in the dry wadi that had been code-named Whirlwind.

As the team progressed toward Whirlwind, Slater weighed some new options that had presented themselves in light of recent developments.

Originally SLAM had planned to hole up for the next fourteen hours of daylight before moving on the strike target and taking it down. But as the FAV rolled across the crusty northern Iranian desert, Slater realized that somewhere in Mukhabarat or army Intelligence headquarters in Tehran a guy in a uniform was sticking pins into a map hanging on a wall.

Those pins would represent the last known positions of the two Iranian motorized patrols that had been unlucky enough to cross SLAM's path. Putting himself in the hypothetical Iranian Intelligence officer's shoes, Slater knew exactly what he would do in light of these facts. He would concentrate new patrol activity within a hundred-kilometer radius of the areas of contact, then work out from that zone in a tightly controlled search grid.

This search activity would commence with first light, Slater knew, just as he knew with certainty that it was coming. To believe otherwise would be to accept a logical fallacy with potentially disastrous consequences for himself and his two men.

Only one option made any sense in light of this data. Slater knew that they had to move on Omar-7 as quickly as possible. If SLAM waited until the night of strike day three to move, there might not be a second chance to hit the target.

Slater checked his Tag-Huer wrist chronometer, consulting one of the three faces whose digital sweep hands indicated zulu, local and Washington time respectively.

Zulu time was 0237 hours, local was slightly earlier, and in Washington they would just be getting back from lunch, probably a little hung over.

"Raise Playboy on the Satcom," he said to Hawke.

"What's up, boss?" Hawke asked, though having mulled over the situation, he'd already figured it out.

"Slight change of plans," Slater told him. "We're gonna hit the target a.s.a.p. I want a go/no-go confirm and an ETA on our extraction."

Hawke began unshipping the Satcom unit, informing Bishop of what was happening as Bishop helped him set up the two modules of the rig. Minutes later Hawke told Slater that they had a confirm on the strike and that extraction arrangements were already under way with an ETA for SLAM at the extraction site Dreamland of six hours.

"Okay," Slater said, checking his weapon's ammo supply and wishing he'd had sufficient time to give it another cleaning to rid it of the omnipresent fine desert grit. "Let's get it on."

THROUGH THE GREEN electronic view field of his NVGs, Mason Hawke looked beyond the long black barrel of the .50-caliber Barret to the gleaming white reactor dome of the Iranian nuclear-weapons plant in the distance.

Five minutes earlier, Slater and Bishop had gone over the fence and were now inside the Omar-7 complex. Bishop carried on his back the submegaton nuclear device with which they hoped to blow the reactor to cinders.

Hawke's role in the op would be to cover his buddies' flanks if they retreated under fire. Whatever the nature of their extraction from the reactor complex, the next step would be to make tracks out of the nuclear blast zone as quickly as possible.

With a blast yield of about four and a half kilotons, the nuke was just powerful enough to raze the complex. Due to its carefully engineered construction, it was clean enough to produce minimal radioactive fallout. However, to ensure against a Chernobyl effect or a worst-case China Syndrome, proper placement of the backpack nuke was of critical importance.

As much as it was desired by the Joint Special Forces Command to put Omar-7 out of commission, SLAM had received very specific and detailed instructions regarding restrictions for arming the bomb's fuze.

If the SADM could not be placed correctly, the mission was to be scrubbed, even if that meant exposing the fact that a covert strike against a nation not at war with the United States had been sanctioned at the highest operational echelons.

Even if it meant sacrificing the lives of Slater and his men.

There were certain lines that men of conscience were not willing to cross, and one of those was in poisoning the environment with radioactive fallout. The strike would be clean or it would not go down; such were SLAM's orders.

While Hawke manned the Barret at his lonely outpost on the high ground outside the nuclear facility, Slater and Bishop had crossed the compound and were preparing to enter the weapons-fuel-processing plant.

Activity levels were low here, and the two guards that Slater and Bishop had taken down with sound-suppressed 10 mm autobursts beyond the fence perimeter would not be found for a while.

Briefed in advance on the precise points of egress from and ingress into the Iranian facility, the two men knew exactly where to enter the compound.

Porting an H&K MP/5-10 Slater stood lookout as Bishop used an electronic descrambler to break the code on the electronic lock that secured the heavy security door to the reactor complex.

The descrambler flashed the entry code in seconds, and Bishop punched it in, pushing inside with Slater a moment later, then slowly nudging the door closed.

No longer wearing NVGs, the two covert strikers moved down a sterile corridor whose walls bore directional signs in Farsi, Arabic, English and French.

Aware from their briefing in Riyadh that security cameras were posted throughout the complex, they negotiated the corridor with caution, using the moments between the cusps of the cameras' side-to-side pan to break from wall-hugging positions and move singly around several D-shaped corridor bends.

Within minutes Slater and Bishop reached the corridor ring's access zone at which was located a security checkpoint. Here the two men donned gas masks and placed the H&Ks on 3-round-burst mode.

Stepping quickly from concealment, Slater and Bishop snapped tight 10 mm burst patterns into the chests of four sentries, quickly terminating them.

They pushed quickly through the doors bearing restricted-area warning signs and swept into the heart of the facility's technical control areas.

A few technicians manned the control instruments that monitored the action of hundreds of gas centrifuges clustered along the floor of an enormous chamber, each separating out highly radioactive plutonium from lighter and less radioactive nuclear components.

Slater flung nerve-gas grenades into the control room. The gas dispersed quickly and went to work almost instantly, paralyzing then killing the technicians who had been performing various monitoring duties around the room. Bishop made sure that two who were near the exits as the gas was spreading were taken down by 10 mm autofire before they could escape.

When the control room had been sanitized, Slater stood watch as Bishop unslung the nuke pack from his shoulders and placed it against the control room's south wall.

The techs had calculated that a blast epicentered there would dump tons of rubble from the dome into the heart of the reactor, completely burying the nuclear fuel rods from which the base product originated.

Bishop armed the nuke by removing the explosive wave generator, or EWG, from the device's safe well and nestling it in the arm well until the transducer plate on the bottom of the EWG was held fast by the locking cams of the arm well. When he completed the first phase of siting the SADM, he turned the timer dials for a twelve-minute delay and signaled to Slater that it was time to hustle.

In only minutes, a cataclysm not seen in those parts since Sodom and Gomorrah would set the night afire.

30

Slater and Bishop's extraction from the demo site proceeded without mishap. It was almost too easy, in fact.

It soon got hard, though.

Having exited into the facility's compound, they were breaking toward the base perimeter when two sentries scheduled to relieve their comrades on duty found the corpses of the guards who had been taken down on penetration.

Smelling the telltale rotting-fruit odor of nerve gas as he neared the facility control center, one guard quickly backtracked and headed for the nearest security phone.

Unlocking it, he placed the handset to his ear and began recounting what he'd seen through fitful coughing. Despite only the faintest whiff of the largely dissipated gas, he was having difficulty breathing.

Slater and Bishop did not have enough time to escape the base perimeter before the base would go to full-alert status in three to five minutes.

Two thirds of the way to the perimeter fence, sirens began howling while helium-arc security lights posted on twenty-five-meter stanchions winked on, bathing the perimeter in a flickering white light.

"Shit, we've been made," Slater said to Bishop as his hand went to the AN/PRC-3000 comset nestled in the radio pouch of his load-bearing suspenders and depressed the send button. "One to Three. Magnet Drummer. Repeat. Magnet—"

"—DRUMMER," Hawke heard Slater's gravel voice in the earbud of his commo headset from his position behind the Barret, recognizing the team's prearranged Mayday code.

"Hoo-ah, hoo-ah!" Hawke shouted over the PCR, already scrambling behind the wheel of the FAV, which stood by with its motor idling. "Check your six. You see greased lightning, that'll be me."

Putting the rig in gear, he cannonballed out of the wadi, the vehicle's great momentum shooting him over the lip of the sand pit as he bounced along the crusty terrain toward Omar-7's hot perimeter.

Above the roar of the FAV's powerful six-cylinder engine, Hawke heard the deep, steady thudding of heavy-caliber automatic weapons. Glowing tracer rounds angled down from the two crow's nests at either end of the base toward the two figures pinned down near the perimeter.

A few seconds of putting the pedal to the metal, and Hawke had highballed the FAV to only a few meters short of the perimeter fence. There he brought the vehicle to an abrupt halt.

On the other side of the fence Slater and Bishop stood back-to-back in a defensive position, throwing wildfire from their 10 mm H&K SMGs at the two crow's nests where Iranian troops were cycling out lashing streams of .50-caliber steel.

Reaching into a deep canvas pouch slung behind him, Hawke grabbed the multiple launch AT-4 rig that he'd prepared for quick deployment in just such a situation.

The four HEAT rounds were armed in their tubular containers, and the launcher's aiming sight was already retracted. The rounds were mere trigger pulls away from hot launch.

Hawke's first round punched a hole in the perimeter fence, carving out a pathway as the high-explosive munition fused and exploded.

By now the troops in the crow's nests had swung the barrels of their heavy guns around at the new threat and were cooking off rounds at Hawke while spitting out brass at a fantastic pace to match the speed of the cycling steel.

Hawke loosed a second Quad-LAW round at the crow's nest on the left in answer to this assault fire. The round went skyrocketing through the air and hit the crow's nest dead on, just beneath its square decking.

A blinding flash lit up the night and the explosion echoed through the desert as a monster fireball ballooned skyward. The top of the crow's nest had been smashed. It careened to earth in a hellish cascade of flaming, smoking fragments.

As bullets from the single surviving guard tower whined down and punched up the sand nearby, Hawke swung the man-portable launch tube up toward it. Acquiring the target, he triggered off a third HEAT warhead.

Like the others, this projectile went whooshing through space. It struck the tower just beneath the base of the crow's nest, blowing it to smithereens and silencing the machine gun that had been saturating the ground with fire.

Slater and Bishop were now staging a fighting retreat toward the FAV. They relegated to second place the call of their instincts that urged them to run helter-skelter for the vehicle. In the first place were the demands of fieldcraft, which dictated that they move in a series of short sprints, using their SMGs to suppress the small-arms fire from troops on the ground.

With the facility's machine-gun towers no longer a threat, Hawke moved the rear of the FAV and swung the .50-caliber Barret around in a ninety-degree arc. It was locked and loaded and ready to crank out its lethal heat.

Triggering the Barret, he sent fire lashing out across the base compound to suppress the ground troops who had taken up protected fire positions, permitting Slater and Bishop to cover the last few meters of ground toward the FAV.

Hawke's two teammates reached the vehicle moments later. Bishop jumped behind the wheel while Slater hefted up the LAW launcher and fired the last round at the pockets of fire on the base perimeter. Bishop floored the accelerator, and the FAV screamed away from Omar-7 at full speed.

Bishop kept driving as Slater consulted his wrist chronometer, which was synchronized with the SADM inside the base control room. The numbers were running down quickly. There was not much distance left to cover before the covert specialist team reached safety because the nuke was relatively clean, but they did not have much slack time.

"Now, out!" Slater hollered, realizing that only seconds remained before the SADM went critical. He needed to get himself and his crew behind the shelter of boulders to protect themselves against radiation in the initial seconds of the blast. After that they could move again.

Bishop, Slater and Hawke scrambled from the FAV and donned tinted goggles to protect their eyes against the nuclear detonation flash. Then they hugged rock and waited for the detonation flash that would signal the nuclear explosion.

Moments later the SADM's kryton switches attached to the explosive shell surrounding its core of plutonium 238 detonated at precisely controlled microintervals, compressing the fissionable material to a third of its original size, thereby bringing the plutonium to the point of critical mass.

That sparked a chain reaction, resulting in a violent nuclear explosion. All hell broke loose in a moment of thunderous noise and fiery blast.

The Iranian nuclear-processing facility went up in a mushrooming fireball, then an obscene toadstool of flame sprouted from the shattered desert floor to light up the night with brightness strong enough to blind and thunder loud enough to deafen.

High above the earth, a variety of satellites from Keyhole photoreconnaissance platforms to Lacrosse radar imaging satellites to Big Bird infrared sensing units were registering the explosion, transmitting the real-time telemetry data to NSA ground stations across the globe.

Down on the ground, hands over their ears, the SLAM team felt the nuclear shock wave rumble through the earth below them. The fierce concussion blast came seconds after the thudding boom that made their ears ring even though covered.

Although they were familiar with all types of conventional munitions, the explosion of a nuclear weapon was like nothing they had experienced before. Powerful as it was, this tactical nuke was a mere toy compared to even a single warhead carried by a Mirved ICBM, each of which might pack twenty times the wallop of the SADM.

Soon the desert was silent and dark again. Deal Slater issued orders for the strike team to climb back into the FAV and move out of the area at speed. They proceeded at full velocity toward the RV point to the south.

SLAM reached the site hours later and used an IR strobe to signal their readiness to extract. In minutes, the *Arlington,* a Los Angeles-class submarine that had surfaced a while before, acknowledged the strobe with an IR strobe of its own.

U.S. Navy SEALs came ashore in a Zodiac with near-silent motors to take them to the sub. They did not often find themselves in awe of many men, but the three SLAM specialists they were ferrying to the *Arlington* were exceptions to the rule.

They proceeded in respectful silence toward the exposed conning tower where the sub's skipper and first mate were watching the extraction through binocular NODs.

Soon Slater, Hawke and Bishop were aboard the *Arlington,* which, decks awash, promptly disappeared beneath the waters of the Persian Gulf to run silently and deep, leaving the region as nuclear fires continued to burn.

EPILOGUE

Damage Assessments

EPILOGUE

Colonel Sammi Esfandir watched from the safety of the Augusta EH-101 helicopter high above the former Omar-7 reactor complex. The Augusta circled like some gigantic steel bird unable to accept the loss of its former nest.

Surprisingly the desert environment had been little affected by the nuclear detonation. According to experts who studied the blast site, everything out from the epicenter to an approximate distance of six hundred meters would be radioactive for hundreds of years, and a containment cap would be needed.

It seemed ironic to the colonel that the Iranians would be forced by these circumstances to construct a kind of monument in the desert to the folly of their imperial designs. The Japanese, too, had their monuments to nuclear destruction, as did the Russians, and both had at one time or another entertained similar grand imperial designs.

That the Americans had committed this strike was beyond question, as was the fact, lamentable to his nation's leaders, that the commandos responsible for this most ambitious covert ground strike had escaped.

Despite all of this, Esfandir's sympathies were solidly with the Americans.

In 1979, when the Islamic revolution swept away the shah and replaced the old monarchic regime with a theocracy presided over by the Ayatollah Khomeini and his fanatical clerics, the colonel had been a staunch believer.

But in eight years of war with Saddam Hussein's Iraq, hundreds of thousands of his countrymen were slaughtered like vermin in the desert. Entire generations of his people were wiped out like flies to perpetuate the power of the fanatic theocracy. When he saw this, Esfandir's revolutionary zeal had been replaced by an overwhelming disgust.

Recruited in place in the late 1980s while on a liaison mission to PLO headquarters in Tunis, Tunisia, the colonel was now an agent in place for the Central Intelligence Agency.

He would file two reports on the aftermath of the nuclear explosion.

One version, for the consumption of the Iranian military establishment, would be full of invective against the "Great Satan" and pledging renewed hostilities against the despised enemies of the Iranian mullahs.

The other version would be written in code and deposited at a clandestine message drop in the heart of Tehran, from which it would be retrieved by CIA ground assets, decrypted and flashed to the Agency after the original was destroyed.

"I have seen everything required," Esfandir told the pilot. "Return to base at once."

"Terrible damage, isn't it, sir?" asked the pilot earnestly.

"We will make those who are responsible pay," he told the young man, in whose eyes Esfandir saw the light of revolutionary zeal that had long ago faded from his own. "Have no doubt of that."

It was just as well that the pilot did not see the flicker of a smile that played over Esfandir's lips. Nor did he grasp the double meaning of his words as he went aft to the crew compartment as the chopper swung around and headed back to Tehran.

THE MAN WHOM some called the Jackal made the final preparations in Cyprus for what he hoped would be a long trip.

Carlos would have to move quickly. That would pose no problem, though. He had been hunted before and had long since learned to live on the run.

In the business he was in, today's patrons often became tomorrow's enemies sooner or later. The communist Chinese were offering asylum to the right parties bearing the right connections. Carlos was fortunate to be one of these privileged few.

His former clients and erstwhile protectors, the Iranians and Libyans, would not catch him where they thought he was. He had left Tehran by a pre-planned escape route the moment word had reached him regarding the destruction of Omar-7.

The Jackal was always one step ahead of everyone else, as he had always been. It was a talent for survival that one was born with, and one he possessed in abundance.

"Enjoy your trip, your holiness," the Alitalia ticket agent said as she handed the old priest in the vestments of the Greek Orthodox church his tickets bearing a red seat-assignment sticker that indicated the no-smoking section.

"I assure you I will," replied the Jackal with a smile. "Peace be with you."

Feigning the feebleness that usually accompanied the old age that his long gray beard and lined visage suggested to onlookers, Illich Ramirez Sanchez walked toward the boarding ramp of the jet that Carlos had no doubt would carry him safely to his journey's end.

Inner-city hell just found a new savior—

JAKE STRAIT

BOGEYMAN

by FRANK RICH

Jake Strait is hired to infiltrate a religious sect in Book 3: **DAY OF JUDGMENT.** Hired to turn the sect's team of bumbling soldiers into a hit squad, he plans to lead the attack against the city's criminal subculture.

Jake Strait is a licensed enforcer in a future world gone mad—a world where suburbs are guarded and farmlands are garrisoned around a city of evil.

A struggle for survival in
a savage new world.

JAMES AXLER

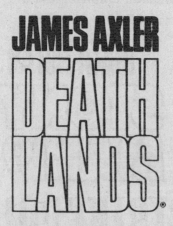

Deep Empire

The crystal waters of the Florida Keys have turned into a death
zone. Ryan Cawdor, along with his band of warrior survivalists,
has found a slice of heaven in this ocean hell—or has he?

Welcome to the Deathlands, and the future nobody planned for.